I Think of Warri

A JOAN KAHN BOOK

I THINK
OF WARRI

Robert J. Attaway

Harper & Row, Publishers
New York, Evanston, San Francisco, London

FIRST EDITION

Library of Congress Cataloging in Publication Data
Attaway, Robert J.
  I think of Warri.

  I. Title.
PZ4.A884Iat [PS3551.T75]   813'.5'4   73–14305
ISBN 0–06–010169–5

"My father, a wise and grave man, gave me serious and excellent counsel against what he foresaw was my design."

Daniel Defoe, *Robinson Crusoe*

"But your duty to your parents, hussy, obliges you to hang him. What would many a wife give for such an opportunity!"

John Gay, *Beggar's Opera*

"It is also possible that one day he may rebel against our ideas, our way of life, and try to be himself."

Georges Simenon, *The Train*

"It was a blow struck against the Party. It was a political act."

George Orwell, *1984*

one

I AM NOT altogether certain that my birth was a good thing, for myself or for anyone else. Nonetheless it's always been my opinion that suicide should not be embraced too hastily. Death in general seems highly inadequate, and I refuse to accept it as a way out. Certainly there is no such thing as an immortal soul, at least not in any traditional sense, and I no longer speculate about that possibility. But I do concern myself with the problem of existence, life as it manifests itself to our eyes and our ears and our touch. And it is within that framework that I seek a personal harmony with the world. People who concern themselves with the purpose of birth and the meaning of death seldom do any good for the living. More often than not they pervert living.

My name is Henry Christopher, but you should call me Christopher. When I was quite young I decided that I didn't like the name Henry and I stopped using it. This little fact is important. It is an example of the way I do things.

My family was white and middle class, and we had a fine home on the outskirts of an eastern city. Childhood was typical.

When I was small I wondered how my father could be such a wise man. When I was older I wondered how he had managed to become so stupid in a few short years. His disintegration never reversed itself. I neglected thinking about him for the most part, except for one brief moment—at his funeral. I looked at the insane artificial sleep that is the mortician's craft and I found myself sobbing with short gasps of emotion. It was nothing more than the realization that he had been, in fact, my father and that this was all there was. Death. He wouldn't be anything anymore—not father, not friend, not enemy.

I was still young when I realized that I would have to be different—that I would have to make a clean, drastic break from that neosuburban background or I would never be whole. Nothing impressed me as being more nauseating than the usual route toward adulthood which most of my classmates would follow. School, work, wife, house, car, kids. It would have been too mundane a path for me to take. I wouldn't have been able to justify it to myself.

Instead I became a merchant seaman, led on no doubt by the shallow clouds of romanticism that seem to surround such a life. Harvard undergraduates will chuckle at the naïveté of this, but such sophisticated disdain is not unlike the death rattle of the suburban routine itself. Both finally reflect the same passive mentality.

But being a sailor is a lonely business. That is the negative factor and there is no doubt about it. You travel across the sea, but you do not erase that awful aloneness. You visit Alexandria, Marseilles, perhaps even the "Isles Beneath the Winds," but it's still the same. A beautiful blue sky and a full warm breeze do not change it. The violence and spray of a storm do not quench it. The women and wine of a port do not smother it. It lurks behind the camaraderie of fellow crewmen; it is inside of you, and it is there that it haunts you.

A seaman, like a tramp, is always on guard against this, yet he ultimately has to face it. It is his old enemy, but he cannot kill it. For reasons best known to himself he is willing to live with it, and keep the sea.

Experienced seamen like to sit around and downgrade the whole business. They will tell you that it is a miserable life, that they can recommend it to no one, that no son of theirs will ever be a sailor. But if you interrupt and ask why they stay with it, why they sometimes try to leave only to come back to it, they can only answer with a few illogical excuses. The fact is that it's a bug which never lets go. You take this trip once and you're never the same again. It's permanent.

People don't write sea stories anymore. Sailors still sit around and talk, but there aren't any tales anymore either. Mostly sea stories were always half faked, but today a cruise is routine and predictable and to add any of that old-fashioned adventure stuff would be outlandish. I would be the first to admit it, but let us not ignore what the modern sailor *does* see. I do not mean as prophet or survivor, but as visual, physical journeyman. That part of sailing hasn't changed at all. Indeed, it cannot change, cannot die—for it to do so the fabric and mystery of human experience would have to die with it.

But these sailors, these modern sailors, have more of a proclivity for irony than for romance, and this is where I differ. Throughout the years I tried to keep my romanticism. I could never successfully let go of old myths and old dreams. Mixed with this conservatism was a wild man at the other extreme, adopting new dreams and new myths as casually as the shoe fit, so much so that harmony was impossible. And perhaps it was this intention to keep holy and meaningful a time-spread series of dreams that made me react so harshly against the imperfections of physical fact. If I had been more passive, maybe I wouldn't have rebelled so thoroughly. As it was, I denounced everything associated with my native culture.

The life which took me around the world on a dozen different ships only hastened this rejection. Glimpses of foreign ports heightened my distaste for my home country. Actually it no longer seemed to me that I had any particular home—certainly no home amid the strife and bigotry, the businessman conformity, the clean materialism of modern America. Nor did the movement of my occupation allow me to find a substitute. In those days I was little more than a constant tourist.

Finally I crumbled. My political philosophy oscillated rapidly between communism and anarchism. I became a walking bomb, hating, sickened and outraged by American society and its logical by-product, the crudity of the American public. I took the only alternative open to me. I escaped.

two

THAT GODFORSAKEN PLACE. How many blank days and how many drunken Fridays. Endless afternoons thinking that—sitting in a sun chair at the club or at a wooden table with rain pounding on a tin roof.

During those blank days, it was the common burn that boiled beneath our words. It wasn't our cliché bitching that stuck with us. It wasn't the exasperation, the superficial hatred. It was the prolonged shock. It was the hurt. It was the difference between this culture and our own which got to us inside. But we did not want to say that then. We did not want to admit it. We certainly did not want to believe it.

The way we think about it now is different. And because we never easily admitted believing our shock, we are quick to verbalize our present love. Sometimes we examine the transition. We try to pinpoint the time and place that reversal happened. Change is like that. One wants to itemize the causality behind it. At such and such a point I realized. But one cannot. We all know it was gradual.

Sand earth with ugly open sewer beside the road, unable to

overlook this desecration even when there is red sunset and green palm tree. Yet red sunset and green palm tree linger. Not some phony vacationer's dream, but pictorial stroke for a haunting landscape. And where in that grime, where in that shantytown, where in that noisy labyrinth was the elusive soul that sustained us all? Maybe it was in the chatter of the market. Or maybe it was just the rattle of taxis on potholed streets. Or the mosquito hush of night and the wind in the rubber trees. Africa.

Reality becomes perspective. We think of Warri. It is Nigeria for us. It is Africa for us. But the crosscurrents of our experience bear little relation to photographic fact. We remember our own eyes and our own people, and we call this reality. It was especially ironic for us because we were foreigners and our reality of Warri was mainly the reality of the expatriate. The native city lived and breathed without us. Because of our length of time in the place, we say we know. But we know it only as collective observers. Just the same, our memories constitute a reality as valid as anyone's. We compound this fantasy. We forget the Sea of Steel and we forget Escravoes Base. We see what we want to see, and reality is diminished very little because of this.

Warri. Older than Columbus. But without a sign. A cluttered African port. Deep in the bush somewhere are remnants of the Portuguese. Dead men in America who were brought from it as slaves. The tradition of the Olu. But it is not a place of history. There is no languishing in the past. The chaos is too present. On Market Road, beside the river, laborers scurry with heavy loads for the boats. And neat young men zip by on motorbikes. And young girls buy tight print dresses.

A conglomeration of the native and the European. Until the tribal mix beats itself into gibberish. Warri. A nation in flux. Like the lion who stretches and pits one muscle against the other. Someone should bang on a tin drum, and that would be Warri. Fifty thousand bodies should wrestle together, and that would be Warri. Young girls should be raped on spring beds, and men should weep, and poets should sing. All of these would be Warri.

Perkins used to say that the trouble with American oilworkers was they had never severed their umbilical cords. He was right, but his bitterness gave the judgment a special harshness. He wasn't just another Englishman dismayed at the growing Texan influx—he was one of the very few old expatriates; nearly two decades on the West African coast made him rage at this sudden Americanization. But as perceptive and sensitive as he was, he was still an old man and his thoughts were becoming rigid. He would mop the sweat from his battered red face and repeat the same pronouncements until they were driven thoroughly into the ground.

I often wondered about the status of my own umbilical cord. No less bitterly than Perkins, I censured those who clung to their roots, furies of indignation and disgust at the Texans who vainly brought their Texas with them. But I could not help myself from seeing both sides of the coin. There are certain motherly ties that one can never escape, and perhaps there are others which one should never try to escape. I wondered if I had gone too far.

(Winter was the quietest season. Somber and weary, animation and color asleep. When it snowed there was a brief respite. The first white morning was always the best, because it covered the too familiar yard and street, cleaned our vision. Sometimes long icicles hung from the roof, and we would knock them down with snowballs. Sleigh days on the hilly side streets. But mostly there was the silence. In the dining room we had an old steam radiator which hissed and fogged the windowpane. We often sat there on the sill and waited.)

The determinists argue that escape is fruitless. It is the environment which molds and creates, and our environment follows us forever and never lets go. I can't deny this, but I wonder if it really poses a contradiction. Molded and held or not, do we still not venture forth in a way that is uniquely our own? And isn't the rejection process natural? What man refuses rejection and really lives?

Perkins again: "You Americans are a strange lot. You never give up mommy, but you ignore that she is there. You push your way around the world with infinite innocence; and when the world finally smashes you down, you fail to understand that it could not have been otherwise."

(But the springs infused us with awe and we lingered around the flowers. My sister and I would cut them from beside the house and carry them to school. Bright color and red energy. In the mornings we marveled at the dew on the grass, and we noted the fact passively when our shoes got wet.)

Perhaps what Perkins says about innocence has some complex association with his statements on momism, but I cannot formulate the relationship. I would not care even to examine the root meaning of innocence. I only know that when I rejected my mother, when I stood up and went out to begin my life, innocence propelled me.

(Summer hung static and hot. Massive worlds rose and fell in our play. At evening, before dinner, we would sit in the dust of the yard and watch the dusk. The bell from the ice cream wagon and the shadows of elm trees. Our eyelids were heavy with peace.)

Youth, not childhood, is the real beginning of life. One attacks the world. Seeks to outstrip all limitations. Scorns prudence. Scorns temperance. Scorns the conventions that get in the way of one's temper.

Before my disillusionment, long before my escape, I was just as passionate and just as confident. My first years on the sea fed this passion. It wasn't a question of locality or of society then; it was all a matter of personality. There was no doubt in my mind that I could someday attain the elusive freedom and power that I envisioned as manhood. The increasing depth of my emotions constituted my energy—a mass explosion of lust and love and fear and hatred and pain and pleasure, striving toward an abstract quality of thought and awareness that no insurance agent could ever sell. And I would overcome all obstacles. I would kill any sonofabitch who tried to put me down.

But I could not kill time, and it was time that finally did put me down. My real birth, my youth, surged forward for just so long and then it faded. As I became hollow, I became bitter. It was the bitterness that led to my rejection and my escape. And my escape ended my bitterness.

Night was coming, and with it a fast black wind that made the boat bobble back and forth from its anchor. The choppy waves would hit us and just when we were in the momentum of our roll the line would catch us and jerk us back. I went out on deck and yelled down to bring up the anchor. They brought it up and we rolled freely without the irritation of this metallic restraint.

For a moment I stayed out there against the rail. I did not mind drifting like this in choppy water. Some sort of an elation connected with the steady rocking, the passive boat on a turbulent sea. Time suspended itself, nothing to measure it, no direction, just motion.

I went back inside and cut the rudders to keep us from pinwheeling. There was nothing more to do except wait, so I sat down on the little bunk I had fixed up at the back of the bridge and stared indifferently at the sea outside.

It was not a pretty sunset. The stubby black clouds that moved with the wind made the equatorial night come faster than ever. In the far reaches of the sky, small patches of crimson managed to survive, but otherwise it was like being encased in an inkwell. The black water looked very cold and very violent. I was looking toward the beach, but I couldn't make it out. All I could see was the metal junk of the offshore rigs. The entanglements of pipe from a dozen wells ruptured the ocean's surface.

There was one torch among the mess. This was a false well,

9

where they had hit gas instead of oil. It wasn't worth the expense to market it, so they set it on fire and let it burn itself out. The darker the sky became, the brighter the torch glowed. A thin black pipe that stood out of the sea and spit fire, and always burning. When you got close to it, you heard a roar and felt the heat. And at night you could see it for miles.

The torch reminded me of Pius, and I remembered the first times I'd seen him. Pius Nzekwo, an Ibo tribesman, smooth, black, tall, slender, young. I must have seen him several times before I consciously noticed him. You could not come into Escravoes without passing the point where he stood. The night that I did notice him, really notice him, I was more puzzled than surprised. The vague feeling that he had been there many times before made my wonder more acute.

He stood against the fence at the tip of a long sandbar which ran out from the end of the dock. This sandbar, matched by another at the other side of the dock, formed a natural harbor. It had been fenced in to keep the Africans from swimming and getting in the way of the boats. He pressed against the fence as a panther might press against the bars of a cage.

I didn't even know who he was then. I couldn't see his eyes, but I knew he was looking at the torch. I did not know why. I could see no sane reason for it. But that was the whole thing. He just stood there and stared at it. An erect black figure looking across the ocean to the red splendor where gas quivered and flickered into the heavens.

Remembering that, I found myself gazing just as intently at the same torch. I turned away from it and looked up at Rig 46. It was a couple of hundred yards off the starboard bow. The boat before me was still unloading and I was next. I still thought Big Red was on it then—inside somewhere, in the galley or in his bunk. I knew I hadn't seen him on deck and I wondered if he had any idea that I was coming.

I was getting nervous and I might have used the radio. Don't ask me what I would have said. It was just a sudden idea that maybe I should send him some kind of message, some little warning that would make him wonder—make him sweat and twist. Because one thing was certain: I wanted this fat bastard to suffer before I smashed him. And I wanted him to know why. It wouldn't be good enough just to knock his head in. That would hurt him all right, but it would heal. I wanted to give him the kind of treatment that never heals, some permanent scar that would disrupt his simple, ugly mind so much that he would never be able to put it back in the same order.

But before I got over to the radio, my engineer came in, and I found myself gliding back into the shell of polite propriety. Simpson was gentle and he wouldn't have understood. His temperament excluded any understanding of violent action. Somewhere in his farm boy background, someone had hammered the Bible into him. There were certain things about his morality that years at sea had altered. For one thing he had come to accept that sailors ashore were apt to behave insanely. And his exposure to this company had cultivated an adolescent's interest in physical sex in an otherwise complacent man. Not that he ever went out and got any. Instead he buried himself in paperback books. Even when we were in port he locked himself in his cabin and read about whores and roughnecks and how they got along together. But violence, real violence, other than the nonexistent barroom brawls that were in his books—this he would not have appreciated.

"There's a squall comin', captain." He always called me captain.

I said yes, maybe, it looked like it.

He shuffled across to the map board and eased himself into a chair. He had one of his books with him, and he sighed and stretched for a minute before he opened its soiled pages. When he parked like that, it meant that he would remain awhile. He usually stayed clear of the engine room when we were at sea and roamed instead from one place to another. He would read a bit, then talk, and read again.

"Forty-six," he said, looking at the rig. "We're always tied up at this one."

I grunted.

"Not so bad, though. You eaten yet? There's some pretty good stew down there. Had to fix it myself."

"I'll go later."

"Listen, cap, we gotta do something about this food situation. Two weeks now without a cook. We gotta get one before we go out again."

"I know. I told them about it, but they haven't got anyone right now."

"Well, we gotta get someone."

"We'll get someone in Escravoes," I said. "If not there, then Warri. We're going to Warri next."

He turned his pockmarked face back to his book. He spent so much time getting through each novel that I marveled at his ability to keep track of the things that went on around him. Yet he was a good engineer. And he was good to be at sea with because he never got excited, never caused trouble. He was the solitary sort, a man from the past.

After a while he closed his book and moved to the door. "Been here a long time now."

I said yes, but I wasn't thinking of that. I was thinking that we had been a long time in Africa. It seemed like a lifetime.

If you come to Nigeria as I did, with little knowledge of the country and Hollywood conceptions of the continent, you will probably end the long plane ride feeling a bit apprehensive. In those last few seconds while the plane taxis to a stop, a slight panic tugs at the bottom of your mind. It is like that split-second gap when you have jumped from the diving board and are waiting to hit the water.

When you step from the plane, you are first struck by the intense humidity. There is no place in the United States where the air is so heavy. The weight of it floods into your opening pores. You are immersed in it so thoroughly that your sense of time and place is temporarily lost. Because it is a totally different world, not easily compared to your world before the flight, you adjust yourself slowly to what seems a new dimension. Some vague sensory perception prohibits continuity between past and present. In adjusting yourself to this atmosphere, you become changed.

Why Nigeria? Because it's not San Francisco or New York or London or Amsterdam or Paris. The next best thing to a blind stab at the map—a stab at a blind place on the map. You should also realize that it is grassland—not the green kind that you walk on, but the real thing. An incidental detail? Not at all. A valuable fact.

I stood for a moment beside the plane and watched the yellow light from the distant terminal. Inside the building itself I felt the exhilaration of one who has come to his destination— this along with involuntary dismay at the absence of plastic airport luxuries.

We went through three separate lines. The first was a military search point. Silent black soldiers in green khakis poked about our hand luggage and motioned us on. The immigration and customs lines were less efficient. We had to wait for the officials to appear and prepare for us. Vast frame windows were open to the night, but there was no wind. Worn floors faced ancient overhead fans. Several policemen in gray khaki shirts and British shorts stood quietly to the side. One was white, and his bony legs took you away from his white face—a pale, chalked, drawn face, as if he never saw the sun and never drank water.

(There is a hush about the snow. Can I use your gloves, Chris? Huh? Huh? Can I? Can I use your gloves?)

I collected my luggage from the customs rack, where more soldiers looked on in the background. In the exit lounge I stopped for a moment and looked vacantly out the door. There were a few stools and a counter where a tired barman read a newspaper. For some reason I felt weak. I wanted to sit down, but an immense fascination with this black world held me dumbstruck. It seemed as if all lights and colors were brighter than they should be. I soaked up this new dimension in the same way one satisfies hunger with food. It was more than lights or colors; instead some psychic sensation beyond tangibility.

I flashed and the musty humidity of the room gave way to a strange feeling of comprehension, an automatic reaction, a fleeting, imaginative kind of thought—but unlike any thought I remembered ever experiencing before, for I could not reduce it to language. It was more emotional, more abstract, more fundamental and encompassing than language thought, warm and harmonious.

On the heels of this feeling rushed an avalanche of American images, dead now but clear. Alarm clocks ringing and lost housewives rushing from bathroom to kitchen. A million empty faces—biological beings who negated intellect in a routine existence of food and family and work work work business competition. Paper work and neon lights and starched white collars. Other faces—the racked souls who were not so successful at negating intellect, who soared into a rationalistic universe they could not comprehend, governed by destructive ethics they could not value. Clanging tenseness and cheap hotels and ringed eyes. And the greatest number of all—those in the middle, who understood the powers of intellect and the dangers too, who therefore beat it down to a functional level, suppressing their discontent. Get up in the morning and go to work and play the game, make yourself believe it, concern yourself with baseball scores and pending legislation.

You are a college instructor, you are a junior executive, you are a plumber, a mother, a salesman. You do your particular crap and try to believe it, actually do believe it most of the time. But deep inside somewhere you hate it. You really hate it.

"Hey, you ever seen that little nigger that's always out on the point at night?"

"Yeah, Pius something or other. It's the torch that gets him. They're attracted to light."

"What's his last name?"

"Numumbu. Jiguvu. Mbazero. I don't know. Pushy little mother. He works in the dining room."

"What in the fuck does he do—sleep out there?"

"Shh-it, Red, I don't know. Oughtta see his wife. Sassiest little nigger ass you ever seen."

During the dry season the mornings are very slow and very foggy. From your window it looks like a bad day—an overcast day in late autumn at home, when it has rained all night and intends to drizzle all afternoon. But it is not cool—it is muggy. These thick mornings precede the brightest, hottest afternoons of the year.

(But, Chris, my hands are cold. My hands are cold, Chris. Wet snow rubbing your skin, making it raw and numb and cold.)

I stepped from my cabin and stumbled through the mist to the main lobby. The heat and the fog weren't the only things that made me tense. There was the mystery of what the shroud concealed. Bits and pieces of the world penetrated it here and there. A short palm tree dripping with moisture to my left. A disappearing clay path to my right. I could see to the edge of the compound where the neatly trimmed lawn stopped abruptly against a wall of jungle. Somewhere beyond that were the morning sounds of people. The noise of children playing. The murmur of loud distant conversation. The thud of someone chopping wood. But then I remembered that the past was gone. I became calm and interested. For the first time in several years I was at peace. I was no longer angry.

This realization obsessed me for most of the morning. On one hand was my utter satisfaction at the effectiveness of my escape.

What I disliked about America no longer mattered. On the other hand was the mystery and uncertainty of the life ahead of me. It was a pleasant anxiety, for it foretold of a totally new experience, a second chance at youth.

I ate breakfast alone in an old colonial dining room. Large square windows brought in the white glare of the fog; but the room was not air-conditioned and I felt my shirt stick to my back. Several of the customers were having large quart-sized bottles of beer with their meal, and the idea did not seem out of place.

I packed after eating and returned to the main building. A clerk showed me to a small bar to wait for my ride. As in most of the rooms I'd seen, an overhead fan hung conspicuously from the ceiling. The place was empty except for the bartender and a redheaded man at one of the tables. I sat at the end of the bar where I had a view through the window. The fog was beginning to fade now, and I had a good look at the dusty street outside. Even with pedestrians passing, it still seemed foreboding, but not unattractive.

(Slush along the curbing. Somewhere the crackle of melting ice. Wipe your feet, Chris. Wipe your feet.)

Red woke up and rubbed his eyes, then staggered to the bar. "Whadda you know, hoss? Just in? Where you goin'?"

"Escravoes."

"Escravoes." He belched and scratched the fat that hung over his belt. "Shh-it. It's the worst hole in this country, and this country's full of holes."

I ordered a beer and Red put his hand on my shoulder. With his other hand he scratched his balls. "Escravoes. It's nothin' but a cock-sucker."

"I guess you'd know."

He stood back a little and belched again. "Smart ass, huh? You'll learn."

I met Red later on the plane. We flew to Warri above thick green bush. Sprinkled throughout the jungle were small villages of mud huts and tin roofs. Part of the way we followed the coast. Violent blue surf swept into pure white beach. This coastline, from the air, looked very primitive.

Red slept most of the way. He only spoke to me once and told me that in a couple of months I'd be calling the place a cocksucker too, and praying to get back to Texas or Mississippi or wherever it was I was from. I told him I didn't think so. And I added, to myself, that I had come there to get away from bastards like him.

Simpson left the bridge and I got up from the bunk and stretched and lit a cigarette. Far away somewhere, beyond the blackness, stretched that same white beach I had seen from the air. I wished I were there, in the sun, away from any living creature. I didn't think about the radio now. The idea of giving Red a warning seemed bad. But I thought about being on a beach.

The closest beach was Escravoes, but there wasn't any surf there and Escravoes was not the kind of beach I imagined. Sometimes I was a bit impressed by Escravoes and at other times I had fun there, but nothing about it made me dream.

They built Escravoes for the oilmen. When they started hitting with the offshore wells, they needed a base—a supply point and administrative center. The mouth of the Escravoes River was the most logical place. There was nothing there in those days except an Itsekiri fishing village and a long sandbar island which seemed tailor-made for such a purpose. One day the fishermen saw a parade of white surveyors dissecting the land with their instruments; and then before anyone really understood what was going to happen, they moved in with the bulldozers and trucks. They cleared the island and built a dock. They erected a power plant and a water system. They constructed massive toolsheds and air-conditioned living quarters. When they were finished, they built a fence around their colony and set to work with the construction of storage tanks across the river.

The boat traffic interfered with the fishermen and soon the masses of fishing sticks, placed close together to trap fish in shallow water, began to dwindle. The village found an easier way to support itself. Two or three dozen huts converted themselves into home-front shops. They brought cigarettes and whiskey and tinned food from Warri and set them on display along the road. Before long the narrow, muddy main street became a legitimate merchant area. For the first time in its history, it was noisy and congested.

The oilmen bought the cigarettes and whiskey and tinned food, and the fishermen got more money than they ever got from the fish. Some took their savings again to Warri and hauled back kerosene refrigerators and radios and record players and thrust themselves into a still more profitable pursuit. A dozen one-room bars opened along the way. The villagers swept their huts and constructed new tin roofs and made places for the customers to sit. And all the time dispensing cold Star beer and keeping Jim Reeves on the phonograph. Then the girls came, and they brought the real money. They came from all over the region with lipstick and tight dresses and modern talk. They stayed in the bars and slept with the oilmen and spent their money on cigarettes and beer and new dresses and folded paper wraps of Indian hemp, which they smoked or sold at a profit to the Americans. The prostitution of Escravoes was complete.

At night the twin cities of the island presented remarkable contrast. On one side was the vast complex of the base with its cold white night lights. Huddled beside it was the dark clamor of music and laughter from the village. White men stumbled from hut to hut—each hut painted now with a big sign in front that said Mexico Bar or Bourbon Street—the men looking from one to another until they found the right place to spend their money and get drunk and get laid and listen to a little Jim Reeves.

Spreading away from Escravoes, toward the open sea, were the grim reminders of their work. This sea of wells and rigs and pipes spread for miles—this Sea of Steel. That was the name I gave it, but the oilmen did not understand how a sailor felt about it. It was just an oil patch to them, a place for them to make the money that they spent in the village. It was a contrived wasteland to me. It disturbed my sense of what should be.

"What did you expect?" Perkins asked me once. "Did you really think all you needed to do was fly over here and all of that would disappear? Didn't you know it'd be worse here than anywhere?"

He was right. I had thought it would be that simple.

I went outside again and flipped my cigarette into the ocean. A cold breeze had come up, and I shuddered a little. I noticed a tenseness in my stomach and for a moment the idea of waiting any longer made me angry.

"I should have done it that first day," I said to myself. "I should have pushed that mother out of the plane."

three

IN SOME RESPECTS those early months were the best. They were not, however, the happiest or the most productive. Moments of loneliness gripped me, held me by the throat as I punished my body with every available excess in an attempt to rid myself of the shock of being in such a different world. I ignored my co-workers and went out of my way to separate myself from the other Americans. It was a desperate, futile method of approach—I sought to devour and embrace the new culture at once, as if my time were limited. I spent my liberty in long nights of whoring and drinking, a circle of debauchery which almost killed me in the hot tropical climate. But I could do it no other way. I had to join their way of life—and if I was confused, beat, sick and offensive, I was nonetheless calling the shots the way I saw them.

Despite this hectic and horrible expenditure of energy, the early period still retained a feeling of magic. It was the beginning of the dry season, and the tempo of Nigerian life boomed outward after months of rain-soaked hibernation. I was intensely fascinated by what seemed a most sensuous and haphazard society. In this people decades removed from primitiveness there nonetheless remained a lust for the earth, for the flesh, for the good life that blared constantly in their high-life music—a noisy, almost Latin American sound of amplified guitars and brassy horns and hollow, resonant talking drums—mambolike rhythms bursting from radios along the streets of Warri, rising toward night sky in open-air dance halls, echoing off the walls of palm wine bars. Most expatriates considered Warri a rathole. But I liked the commotion, the congestion, the looseness, the rough-hewn urbanization, the hordes of half-naked children who screamed at a white man as he passed—not from hostility or admiration or fear, but just because he was white. See white man, yell white man. A simple, expressed openness which characterized Nigerian life.

I had a regular run, ferrying supplies from Warri or Burutu to Escravoes and the offshore rigs. Sometimes we were on the move for a week or two at a time. Or maybe we laid over for a night at Escravoes. Every three weeks or so we had a few days in Warri. I didn't know much about Warri then. I only knew that it had the forbidden, foreign quality I sought—the night streets of that city embraced me with the tender, violent compassion reserved for the doomed or the daring. I could not fathom that it was a real home for so many people, for I fled to it with the jaundiced, weary eyes of one who has seen too much and is happy to be swallowed in a place that most would consider a sewer.

By contrast Escravoes made me uncomfortable. I could not roll up in my bunk with a book like Simpson, nor could I lose myself in the oilmen's bars of the village. I stayed aloof from these places when they were crowded. Instead I strolled to the outskirts of the bush. At times I parked in a bar, but invariably something happened that made me leave.

One night I spent the early evening in the Mexico Bar. It was the only place in the village that had the kind of music I wanted to hear. They had Jim Reeves and all the others too, but I was the only customer and I made them put on something different. I didn't feel like going with one of the girls. I relaxed alone, drinking, enjoying the sound.

All of this was interrupted when a group of Americans came in. Among them was the big redhead. He gave me a nod, and a few minutes later Jim Reeves was back on the phonograph. I might have stayed just the same, but something happened which made me want to get out. One of the prostitutes was sitting on the arm of Red's chair soliciting for a drink. He took his cigarette and burned her on the arm. She bounced up and let fly with a string of obscenities, while Red and his companions roared with laughter.

So I left and walked away from the village. I avoided the other bars, stepping through the shadows between mud huts until I was alone in the bush where I followed a clay path that led to the beach. It was a bright night and I could see for a good distance. I thought nothing, or next to nothing. I knew the path would lead me to a dead end at the water's edge and I knew too that there was nothing for me to do there. But there was a very real sense of relief as I got farther away from the village. I stopped once for a moment, but the hush of the forest scared me a little and I moved on at a fast pace. Walking kept the fear away, yet still allowed me a sensation of closeness with the trees and brush around me.

It didn't take long to reach the water. It was a wide, sloping beach with a full view of the port and the open sea beyond it. Stepping onto the beach immediately brought me away from nature and the curious, cleansing sense of isolation I had experienced on the path. I wanted to walk up the beach, upriver, away from the port, and I started in that direction, but I soon discovered that the beach narrowed rapidly until it disappeared altogether, leaving only thick brush and mangrove to meet the black water. I turned then and walked toward the port. The huge gas torch was visible out to sea and the whole horizon in front of me seemed to flicker with this redness, as if there were no sky at all, only a screen played upon by magnified Halloween lights.

I walked until I came to the fence beside the harbor. This was on one jutting side of the harbor and was not well lit. The white dock lights were behind me to the left and the jutting sandbar tip of the harbor to my right. There was no way into the dock from where I stood without climbing the fence, and I started to do so when I noticed someone standing at the edge of the sandbar. He was near to me, but apparently hadn't seen or heard me coming.

It was the Nigerian, the one they talked about. I hadn't yet learned his name. He stood motionless and looked seaward at the torch. The red glare reflected on him and I could see one side of his face. He looked very young, but rigid like a statue or a guard on duty. And he looked at the torch with a kind of rapture and attention that sent chills through my blood. I felt embarrassed seeing him so closely, as if I had interrupted someone making love. For no logical reason I watched him as demonically as he watched the torch.

I did not climb the fence. I turned and went silently back the way I had come, finding the path and passing the bush and the village until I had circled back around to the dock. When I got on board I went up to the bridge and looked for him along the fence, but he was gone.

Early in December, before the dry season becomes really hot, there is a brief time known as harmattan. It lasts only a few weeks at the most and is thought of as a season in itself. It is very dry during this time and somewhat cool, for the sky is overcast with a light reddish haze similar to smog in appearance. This is actually dust from the Sahara which the annual winds blow south. It is not as bad as smog, but the dryness cracks your lips and bothers your throat. Nonetheless, the discomfort is more than compensated for by the coolness, the autumnal feeling, the single time of the year when the West African coast is crisp at night.

My first harmattan impressed me especially, for I was still not used to the muggy heat and this period of relief brightened my outlook. It was during this time that I decided to get an apartment in Warri. I would only be able to use it a few days each month, but I wanted a place away from the ship for my days off.

I rented a small, noisy, second-floor flat which overlooked one of the town's busier streets. There is little privacy in Nigerian life, and this more than anything thrust me into the belly of their society. There was a constant din of radios and children and women chattering, late to bed and early to rise, and this racket made it hard to relax. But it did not take long to get used to it, until I actually liked the uproar I was a part of. The neighbors were aggressively friendly, and soon I knew most of the people in the building.

There was a front balcony where I spent much of my time. I had a week's liberty around Christmas, and I spent it sleeping and drinking and standing on that balcony watching the constant flow of traffic in front. It was very pleasant during those harmattan days. I had a good view up and down the street. Across the street, to the right, were the walls of a federal prison, but next to that was an open field which extended for some distance, with a few palm trees and a rice field behind it. Standing there I realized I had passed the initial shock that I experienced during my first weeks in Nigeria. I had less and less need to resort to wild drunken nights. Instead I was settling in with a certain amount of peace and a certain satisfaction at having found a new place to live.

It was because of the apartment that I met Perkins. I had finished breakfast and was reading on the side balcony just outside my bedroom. The balcony extended all the way around the building, and this side spot was the quietest and most private. From it I saw the rooftops, all tin, of a dozen one-story flats, very close together, which extended on up the block. The other side was not as good. You looked directly into the three-story apartment building next door. And the front, because of the noise from the street, was no good for reading. I was disturbed anyway. I had a part-time cook and "houseboy" named Peter, a tall, silent man much older than myself, and I had only read a few pages when he announced a visitor.

The caller looked like someone from the steaming reels of an old jungle movie. He wore crumpled white slacks and a soaking white shirt which stuck to his skin even in the relative coolness of the season. He was not fat, but rather large and lumpy-looking just the same. Above his sweating, ungraceful bulk perched a beet-red face with large, protruding features and a shock of graying hair.

He pulled up a wooden chair and sat down before I had time to say a word. "Perkins," he said, then turned his eyes to the horizon and breathed heavily, a rasping way he always breathed, as if he were catching his breath. "American, aren't you?"

I said I was and introduced myself.

"Oh, I know your name all right. They told me you'd moved in." I had no idea who the "they" was, and at the time it somehow seemed impolite for me to venture this or any other direct question.

He waved his hand vaguely toward the jumbled complex of buildings behind my own. "We're neighbors. This was all open land when I came. They were going to extend the European reservation over here, but it'd have been too expensive to fill in the rice field." This reservation he spoke of was several blocks opposite the front of my building and was the old name for the white residential area. They were big, expensive houses with large yards; and though the occupants were still mostly white, nobody called it the reservation anymore.

"Unusual to get an expatriate in this section. Couldn't pay most of them to live here. This American riffraff coming in won't touch it either. Myself, I couldn't afford to move to a better place if I wanted to."

He breathed for a few silent moments and extended me a soiled business card. "Henry Perkins. Expert Printing at Unbeatable Prices."

"Came out here with the Ministry of Information, but I was too ambitious. That was it. Got my own shop, two employees now. I wanted to build my own empire, but I never had more than four employees. Printing's a big thing here—handbills, that sort of thing—but no money in it."

Again he paused, for a long time now while he lit a cigarette. "They don't talk to me anymore—the Europeans, I mean. Even at the club they don't. It's all changed. No one knows me anymore, or they know who I am and they think I'm nuts."

He stopped with an air of finality, looked at me critically, then looked away as if it didn't matter one way or the other if I was there.

Nor did he resume talking. For long, awkward moments there was silence. I was waiting for some further comment, but he had given all the explanation he intended to give. We moved inside, where it was more comfortable, and I sent Peter to buy beer.

The conversation never really picked up, never fell into any of the usual moods or patterns that people adopt when they communicate, and I was soon to learn that this disjointed manner was Perkins' natural method of expression. He spoke as if everything he said were a pronouncement, formulated and passed on without plan or ulterior purpose. It was at once honest and distant. For while the words and thoughts were straightforward enough, the lack of overall pattern suggested, it seemed to me, a lack of concern. In retrospect I sense that I was unfair, but at the time I often wondered if he really had anything to say at all.

A few beers brought sweat to my own back; and as they did, they dispelled the nervous silence I had kept outside. I was wondering aloud about the empire he had wanted to build, when he threw it back at me. "We all want the same empires, isn't it? Yourself, you're young. If it's not some private empire you have in mind, then why did you move into this flat?"

"I don't see the connection, but why not live here?"

"It's substandard, for one thing. There are new places along the highway. Tiled and air-conditioned and carpeted. Expatriate places."

"I'm poorer than most of the others."

"Not that," he said. "It's because you're young."

"I'm not so young. I'm not even in the younger half."

He lifted his arm in a peculiar kind of shrug. "That has nothing to do with it."

He was preoccupied with this topic, and every minute or so he returned to it. We had been sitting for over an hour, and every few moments my landlord passed the open door along the balcony. He had no job and he paced around the building most of the day. The building really belonged to his wife, a tremendously large woman who ate snails and spoke no English, and his position in the household was dubious. He had spoken to me only twice, and both times he had been incoherently drunk, for he began taking native gin as soon as he woke up.

Perkins saw him pass. "That man was once a taxi driver." That was all he said about him; but the landlord had sharp ears, and the reference to him must have drifted out. He turned abruptly and entered my apartment.

"Ha, yes. All 'round. Lagos, Benin, Sapele, Ibadan. You see, Mr. Chris'opher, he knows." It was not quite noon. He was still understandable, but very much on the way. "You know Ijoto, Mr. Chris'opher. I was just going. You know. Huh? Just a short time. Huh? Come, I show you."

I didn't know what he was talking about, but Perkins nonchalantly stood up. "Why don't we," he said. "It's just a bar."

It was a dusty three-block walk, on the same street I lived on, past homes and shops, street vendors and screaming kids, carefully treading the edge of the open drain and watching out for the traffic. The Ijoto Hotel—three run-down floors. Not a hotel really. A whorehouse bar. Not an expatriate one. Not a Nigerian one, even—only for the lowest of the low. Truck pushers and motor park boys, the toughs and loiterers who scratched out a living at truck stops and taxi stations. Indian hemp. Rotting chairs. Peeling paint on the walls. The first floor sold palm wine. The second, beer. Quiet and empty during the day. We sat there.

Perkins dreamed of empires. "If that's not it, then what is it? Why not stay in the U.S.?"

"I'd had enough of it."

"You left for no reason? No plans, no alternatives?"

"I had reasons. I left because I didn't want to stay."

"A negative man. And American too. You speak quite well for one, you know. This riffraff, what do they know of the tropics? I knew it was spoiled when the first one came. Oil, they say. They might as well have opened a coal mine under the main market."

Perkins looked at no one while he spoke; he seldom ever looked at you when he talked. Something oddly contradictory about his appearance with his words and the way he said them. He looked seedy, racked by too many years of failure and lonely living in a hot climate. The continuous sweating, the rasping breath, nervous mannerisms as if he were always stealing a moment between distant appointments. Yet his tone of voice was level, self-sarcastic without being self-pitying. It was a bit on the smug side—the kind of tone that might have seemed more appropriate in the mouth of a missionary sipping soda at the club and passing judgment on the problems of a world that he really couldn't care less about.

But he was wrong when he said I had no reasons, only negative motion. At least I thought he was wrong. Nor did I consider the concept of empire in any way applicable. I wanted a foreign home; it was that simple. And I thought I had one. I was becoming pleased with it and the pleasant chaos in which it was set. It was the answer to every man's ambitions and every man's concerns. Not a simple life of simple values and goals, not so open to attack and contradiction. Instead a life of no values, no goals, no purpose—where chaos became harmony, because chaos was the order of the day and nobody suffered from it.

The landlord took no interest in what was said. He was drinking very quickly, mixing stout with regular beer in his glass. He grinned below glazed, boiling eyes and wiped his mouth with his hand, slobbering considerable amounts of the liquid. Despite his wiping, a brown crust formed on his lower lip. But he did not seem to care. He tapped his foot in a complex, unfathomable rhythm and occasionally twisted in his chair, a kind of sitting dance, a rock, or maybe a cha-cha, whatever was happening to his mind.

Perkins took long, slow swallows. "You have no wife. Prostitutes? The people at the club? You must know this place very well before you can be calm here. It's not what it seems. It's a mistake to be calm."

"The people seem easygoing enough."

"I should say they were frantic. Touch-and-go emotions. A government on the rocks. Living from hand to mouth."

"It's an immediate living."

"Is it? I don't know. The immediacy is only a front. It covers the gap between what they want, so naïvely want, and what they have."

The landlord suddenly made the barman put on some music and then came back over and handed me a piece of meat. "Huh? Go on. Bush meat. Congo meat, Mr. Chris'opher. Sometimes. Yes. Are they taking it there? I can. Huh? Not too much."

I chewed the meat, and he moved to sit down, but stumbled and sat on the floor instead. He stayed there, leaning his head against a chair.

Perkins got up and stretched, making the motion to leave. "I must push the point," he said. "Why did you come here? Why did you leave America?"

The landlord jumped up from the floor and looked at me with a straight face. "America. Everyday. Huh, Mr. Chris'opher?" He laughed wildly then and slapped me playfully on the shoulder. Suddenly serious again, he wheeled and stumbled helplessly into the nearest chair, eyes closed.

"I hate America," I said.

"A touch of bitterness, hey?" He left then, and I did not see him again for two weeks.

I stayed a few minutes longer, vaguely uncomfortable but not sure why. I went to the large front window, which faced the street. The post office was directly opposite. Activity. People going, coming, businesslike, things to do, things on their mind. It was the harmattan and it was cool.

I tried to wake the landlord, but he wouldn't budge. The barman, a boy of twelve or thirteen, assured me it was all right to leave him there. He finally arrived back at the apartment that night. There was a great commotion in front. For some inexplicable reason he refused to pay his taxi fare, a shilling. Everyone congregated for the disturbance. He screamed at the driver and made to attack him, but the neighbors held him back. His shirt was torn and he had bruised his forehead in a fall. Much struggle getting him upstairs, stumbling, rebelling, falling on the steps, the driver behind him demanding payment. They finally got him in his apartment and I paid the driver his shilling and the crowd dispersed.

It was the harmattan and it was cool.

The Midwest Inn is on the outskirts of town, on the highway coming in, a Lebanese-owned motel and club. A slick Ghanan jazz group for dining and dancing, in the middle of a forest of rubber trees. You remove yourself from the parties in the dining room and sit in the adjoining alcovelike bar. The bartenders wear bright-green vests. Not a large place and you talk to the people around you. All agree—it is a blank day.

These days seem to happen more often than not, undercutting the pleasantness of adjustment, a series of days with a life of their own. Lethargic, dull, stifling, making you wonder why you are there. No matter who you talk to, you find that it is a common experience. In the middle of a blank day, you forget that there is anything else. Long and empty days. You pity yourself. You are irritated by the Nigerians, by some shortcoming you imagine in them because they are different. You get hostile at the people who yell at you on the street. Contemptuous of the noise, little native mannerisms, provincialities.

So you sit at the Midwest Inn and exchange complaints. Waiting, wondering, killing time. Often these blank days seem like the predominant part of your experience.

It is nighttime in Escravoes harbor. I walk around the deck. The Nigerian is on the point. Impossible not to wonder about him. A little later he comes back toward the dock and sees me on the boat. He walks along the dock where we are tied up. A self-conscious, gentlemanly nod. "Good evening."

"Good evening."

"You work on this boat?"

"Yes."

"Are you the captain?"

"Yes."

He grins exuberantly. "I am working at the base myself. I was looking at the light."

"Yes, I saw you."

"They say it is gas that makes it."

"Yes."

"It is a wonderful thing. They put it there, you know. It wasn't always so."

He shakes his head in glee and walks on, between the warehouses, until he is out of sight.

The expatriate club was officially the Warri Club. During the colonial days it had been the European Club, but now it was simply a club and half of its members were Nigerian. They did not attend much, though, and so it was the expatriate club. A country club of sorts, swimming pool, billiards, restaurant, large bar which opened onto the river.

In my zeal to avoid Europeans, I had as little to do with it as possible. But now and then my apartment or the Ijoto became too cluttered, pushing in on me, destroying any illusion of pleasantness. I escaped then to the club, testimony to the fact that I could not so easily reject what was native to me.

The club itself had nothing to do with Nigerian society. It was its antithesis—a white island disdainfully different from the racket of the Warri streets. One sat in the afternoon and watched the sun go down on the river. At night there were the lights of passing boats and the purr of their motors. There were other activities—films, a library, tennis, tombola, table tennis. I went to the club and I needed it; but it was a complex subculture with rules, factions and an etiquette all of its own making. It was bullshit any way you sliced it.

An afternoon. There is a small group at the bar. Mostly English. The American rednecks are still at work among the pipes and pumps of the oil business. They would be in later, complete with boots and cowboy hats. "Shh-it, hoss, let's get outta this limey place and get laid tonight." "Get a nigger by the ass." "I'm gonna kill me one of these mother-fuckers."

The club people are more circumspect than Nigerians about starting a conversation. But if you are alone at the bar on an afternoon, they will draw you into their conversation, if for no other reason than to find out who you are.

A tall, obnoxious Englishman, thought to be an American sympathizer, is on my left. He calls himself Jeff. "How long have you been here now?"

"Just a few months. You?"

"Five years," he says. "My third contract. Are you on an eighteen-month job?"

"No. I'm here for good."

Momentary pause in the conversation. People look at me sideways.

A big American comes in, looks the group over and approaches me. "Say, can you tell me how I can get invited on board that Swedish ship that's in port?"

I tell him to go on down to the dock and ask. He has rightly sized me up as a sailor, but has mistaken me for one of the crew. Suspect. People who approach sailors this way.

"I tell you it's civil war, that's what it's going to be."

"I agree. You wait. They haven't even started killing each other yet."

"Steward! Steward! Three large beers here."

"Twenty Gold Leaf, steward."

A haze of chitchat. Where am I? Who am I with?

"Red? He'll be in later."

"That old boy sure is onery. Don't take no shit from nobody."

I shut them out of my mind. A vague uneasiness makes me move to a table. It is better there, alone, a nice breeze from the river. Two lives—no, three. A boat, an apartment, a club. Was it naïve to depend on all three for firm footing? Perhaps not. I was, after all, as faceless as the wind itself.

It was late, and we were still waiting to get in. The boat ahead of us must have had a full load; and since it was night, they weren't rushing any to get it off. Theoretically the rigs worked with a full shift around the clock, but the fact is they took it easy at night. It was like an overflow valve—it gave everybody a chance to loosen up.

I went on down and had supper. We had a nice galley, better than most of the other vessels. There was a big table and paneled walls, and it was separated from the cooking area a little so you could sit around when you were free and use it as a rec area. We had good food on board too, and deep-freezes that could hold enough for two months. I guessed they were never full except when they brought the boat over from the States. I was glad I hadn't been the one to do it. It was a thirty-day trip in a vessel this size and pretty rough going.

Eating settled me down a little; and by the time I went back up on the bridge, I was calm and sleepy. Some of the anger had drained out of me. Not the real anger, not the conviction, the intellectual hatred, but the excitement I had created in myself. It would be just as well not to meet Red until I had it back.

We had drifted quite a way from the rig itself, so I started the engines up and brought her closer in. It looked like we'd be there all night so I had the anchor lowered and called it a day. I left the radio on in case they wanted us to come on in before morning and stretched on the bunk. I could not sleep there, though. I told the Nigerian on watch to keep his ear peeled for a call and went on down to my cabin.

It was a closet-sized place, but I spent a lot of time there. I had a few books and a typewriter. Sometimes I sat there for hours with the door shut, just sitting.

I had a hard time getting to sleep, worrying about the morning, how it would happen. With my emotions calmed down, something else slipped in that I didn't want to admit. The more I imagined the morning, the more it came. Just easing into me. It was fear and it would not stop growing.

I had to face it then. I had to say to it: Look here, don't mess me up, don't stop me from doing this because this is something I have to do.

But it is no good talking to it like that, trying to put it down. You have to ignore it, just let it stay there on one side of you. You make up your mind what you're going to do and let the other run its course alone.

Still, it was hard getting to sleep. I wondered about the incomprehensible world that had brought me there, to that time and place. Why? I was so deep in the quagmire that I had no sensible idea. Where did the world stop and I begin? I could maintain no clear perspective. I had shifted perspectives so often that any grasp of the whole was lost in its parts. It seemed that no stance brought me to an end—to satisfaction or conquest. The thought had often occurred to me before and it frequently kept me awake. Sometimes I said to myself, "I have it"—not the answer, but the disease. It is an insight and it has lifted me out of the limited role that accompanies a unitary perception; but it is miserable. I have not been able to synthesize the multiple. Instead I am lost somewhere in the twilight area and it is uninhabitable.

But I knew these thoughts would only get me despair. It was not the proper time to sort them out. I had to put them in that concurrent area along with the fear. What I had to do now was complete the task in front of me. I had to face Red and I had to defeat him, and that was that.

It was a bad night and the boat rolled roughly. All I could do was roll with it, in my bunk, until there was sleep.

A Speculative Look at Perkins

He was born in the sordid guts of Liverpool, and that fact alone had much to do with his leaving England. Perhaps if he had been a Londoner or a country boy, it would have happened differently. He might have become a sophisticated urbanite in one or a gentleman farmer in the other—but there was nothing, nothing at all in Liverpool that gave him much of a berth. His parents were poor, unskilled, and his father suffered from asthma. This too was important, for it trapped him, stunted him in childhood in a way that no human being should be stunted. There was nothing for him to do but suffer, knowing very little about anything else.

The only path to glory in his boyhood slum might have come

through better physical endowment, for what glamour existed along those streets was the glamour of the delinquent and the gang. It was the most available escape. It could enlarge your world. It could even take you out of it. But there was no place for him here either. He was big but he was awkward, and the toughs who seemed so magnificent in that perverted world would have nothing to do with him. He was sensitive by temperament and the peer group rejection only convinced him all the more that he was in the wrong environment.

Education might have provided the escape, but he was hopelessly inept in school. Teachers terrified him and he panicked at every question and test. Undoubtedly he was more intelligent than he appeared, but the fact was he was no genius. This he accepted early in life. He knew that if he could ever use his wits he might pull free of his past; but he knew also that he would have to work at it, that no sheer degree of brainpower would carry him through.

He quit school at sixteen and went to work in a mill. His position there was inferior too, for he was a clean-up man and had little to do with the real work of the place. Nor did he mind too much, for that kind of work seemed little better than what he had.

He had one dream—to leave Liverpool and to leave England. Maps fascinated him, and he imagined exotic corners of the globe and the hospitable life they might hold for him. When he was nineteen, he visited an uncle in Malta. The uncle was not wealthy, but he took an interest in the youth and managed to finance his passage. The visit was an eye-opener of what could be. The colonial world fired his imagination—he would have to be a part of it.

His intention then was to go to London, work, learn a skill, wait for the opportunity to present itself. Then too his uncle promised to help. He stayed in London for three months working at odd jobs. Then his uncle died in Malta and, discouraged and lonely, he returned to Liverpool. He hadn't forsaken his dreams but he wondered if he would ever realize them. His aging father was no longer able to work and it was necessary for him to provide support.

He began as a printer's apprentice in Liverpool, and three years later, with some experience and a little savings, he went again to London. But his education and training provided no easy way into the colonial service; and, now that he was supporting his mother (his father had since died), simple immigration to one of the colonies was impossible. In the face of difficulty, he became lethargic, and for the next ten years he went on working, watching his dreams fade until he himself only vaguely remembered them.

When his mother died, he returned to Liverpool and shortly afterward married a girl he had known for some years. He didn't love her, but he needed someone and he had now resigned himself to an uneventful life. They lived routinely. They had no children. They were firmly a part of Liverpool.

When the war broke out, he tried to enlist. But he now had asthma like his father and he was rejected. He and his wife went to London, where he spent the war working in a government printing plant. The war itself had one significant effect on him —it killed his wife in a bombing raid.

Through some twist, some strange process of the human imagination, he now found that his old dreams were returning. He had to get to the colonies. He realized that the Empire was past its peak, that England and the world were changing. He resented these facts, but the realization that they were true made him panic at the thought that he might get to the colonies only to find that it was too late. The panic finally served his own purpose. It urged him to get going. The war was hardly over when he accepted a printing position in Nigeria.

He had made it. He had escaped from Liverpool.

four

I WAS WALKING the deck at night, bored and lonely, and thinking about these two often experienced conditions. It seemed to me that they frequently went hand in hand, and it occurred to me also that I have always believed in both. Not completely, of course. Friendship and love are better than loneliness, and it is better to be interested and involved than bored. But I've always felt that loneliness and boredom are necessary human things, things to be cherished for what they are worth. Both are forms of discontent and both are negative stances, but the power of negative thinking seems very valid to me. I have sometimes sought loneliness and fostered boredom.

It would be easy enough to ascribe this tendency of mine to some psychological aberration. Or to maintain that my justification of these is a rationalization after the fact, a process for accepting the way of life that has made them mine. But I don't think such a diagnosis is entirely valid. What is boredom but an annoyance with the immediate stimuli in front of us, and how can any man make demands upon life and seek to increase its range and quality without such annoyance? To adopt a style that consistently and gleefully accepts the petty and the fleeting is to squelch higher motivation and all those other effects, some good and some bad, to which the power of reason logically leads.

By the same token, what is loneliness but an emotional and intellectual side effect of coming to grips with the self as it sees itself and must live with itself? If the individual sees himself only in relation to others, then he reduces self to role. But when he is alone and alone long enough to be removed from the immediacy of his public actions, he must survive with and evaluate the inner distillation of his roles, the inner resources that exist apart from public masking, and the rational worth of his own existence. Only then does he fully realize his individuality and his intellectuality, for only then is he painfully aware of these as a movement or pattern apart from gregarious and strictly functional patterns. Again he must separate the trivial from the principled. He must spend frantic amounts of energy in inner reflection, a kind of reflection which would seem necessary simply because it is possible.

So I've often tried to turn pain into meaning, loneliness into growth, boredom into direction. It has put me in a kind of double world. Neither solitude nor social fulfillment can stand alone, and I'm unhappy in either.

We were tied up at Escravoes, but I didn't leave the boat. I wanted someplace to go and someone to talk to, but I rejected those places that were available. This would not have bothered me if I had thought the time was right for being alone. If that had been the case I might have read or listened to music or sat drinking beer in the galley. But the loneliness was beginning to get to me. This was different from the shock and loneliness of my first weeks; those weeks were painful simply because of the radical change in my surroundings. This was a more mellow loneliness, too extreme to be suppressed by prostitutes or booze, yet too intense to be accepted.

I paced back and forth from bow to stern, and this was not

something that I often did. I panicked at the realization that perhaps I had come to a dead end. It was easy enough to say I had emigrated out of the States and that this foreign, racially different culture was my new home. But the immaturity and inadequacy of that simplification was no longer enough. Now that the first violence of adjustment was over, I freely admitted that I liked Nigeria. But the time had come when more than that was needed—more than an apartment and a landlord, more than infrequent conversations with Perkins or expatriates at the club. Something had to spring from the place itself, and I was afraid that nothing was coming.

These doubts were interrupted by the Nigerian. He stood on the dock and faced the boat. I now knew that his name was Pius, for he stopped frequently on his return from watching the torch. I would not have noticed him if he hadn't yelled. "Good evening!" He shouted it like a schoolboy, enunciating four clear syllables. I motioned him to come on board and we leaned against the rail together.

"I've come to greet you," he said. It was a ceremonial statement that he never neglected.

We looked at the harbor. He seemed content with the situation. A slight, amused smile remained on his lips, and his rolling white eyes passed naturally back and forth across the water. From his expression and the movement of these wide eyes, one would have thought some magical, slightly comic sporting event was in progress.

"I like your boat very much," he said. "You have come from Texas?"

"No, from Massachusetts."

He did not try to repeat the name. "That is a good city?"

"It's okay. It's a state."

"I think Texas is bigger."

"Yes."

"But Texas is small to California."

"California has more people."

"We are always hearing of California," he said.

Long pauses separated such bits of conversation. It wasn't easy to make small talk with Nigerians. Unless they were well educated or had spent a lot of time around Americans, they found it difficult to understand your accent and you found yourself talking in an exaggerated tone, very distinctly, in an unnatural syntax. The Nigerian accent itself challenged comprehension, although somewhat less so than vice versa. Native tonal patterns unconsciously superimposed themselves on the more level pattern of English, and aside from differences in idiom, Nigerians sometimes rearranged their sentences to conform to these tones.

"I would like to go to America," he said.

"Why?"

He grinned and gave me an incredulous look. "I should like to work there. The Americans are very good at work. There are many millionaires."

The topic had come up before, and he had seemed genuinely surprised when I told him that I had never met a millionaire. I think he suspected me of lying. He probably thought that I was a millionaire myself.

"I must introduce you to some beautiful girls," he said. "Do you know Nigerian girls?"

"Only hotel girls."

"That is too bad. I will bring you some nice young girls. I have many cousins."

I told him I'd like to meet some.

"I would like to meet an American girl."

I smiled and shrugged.

"But they do not like black men, isn't it?"

"Some do not."

"Do you like black girls?"

"I'd like to know some."

"I will bring some. I like black girls. But you Americans are wonderful, na-wha-o."

In Nigerian English, "wonderful" meant anything from amazing to pathetic. "Why is that?" I asked.

"You have money," he said. "So much. Na-wha. It is wonderful."

Again we were silent. And indeed he did seem to think Americans were wonderful. He saw Escravoes Base differently than I did. His capacity to do so amazed me, for he was well aware of the bigotry of most of the oilmen. And while he seemed continually awed at the Texans' capacity for physical labor under a hot sun, he clearly detested these workers in most other respects. On one of his previous visits he had told me that they did not behave well, that they fought too much and did not like his country, that it was not good the way they spent money. Still, he truly admired Americans and this base that they had erected. Machinery excited him.

"I would like to work on your ship," he said.

I smiled but said nothing.

"I am a good cook. I know the European diet very well."

I told him we already had a cook. This was a lie, since we had been a week without one. But I wasn't in a business mood and felt leery about committing myself so easily.

"If you could see my handwork. I know about your food. I do not cook African chop. That is for women. But I'm a first-class European cook. It is my trade."

"Maybe I'll call you if I ever need a cook."

"That is good. I would like to cook in America someday. When people see my handwork, they will make me a millionaire."

He laughed wildly, enthusiastically, as if it were only a matter of time before this became fact. He left shortly after that, nearly bubbling over with confidence. It was as if some fantastic future lay in front of him and all he had to do was pluck it. There was no doubt and no maybe. If you added two and two, you got four, or maybe more. No evidence to the contrary seemed to bother him.

I wasn't sure whether his visit had brightened my spirits or made me more discouraged. Maybe such optimism was its own reward. Maybe I had never had enough of it and that was why I was alone, in Africa, with nothing of my own except my occupation. Or maybe optimism was foolhardy. Maybe it did make a millionaire or a king at times, but maybe also it was the device that people used to wreck themselves. And if I was wrecked, as I thought that night that I might be, then perhaps it was some exuberant boyhood dream that had caused it all.

I wondered where the dream stopped and reality began. And where fulfillment for both rested.

In an isolated moment when his put-on bitterness weakened and the really deep bitterness inside became visible, Perkins talked about his days in England. His usual attitude was to refer to this period as if it were something of no consequence, something prior to the birth of his real personality. But he knew himself that this wasn't the case. And whether rightly so or not, he looked upon those early days with regret and pain.

"It is not regret at the way they were, though God in heaven knows there is room enough for that. No. It is shame that I feel for myself. And it should be, for if a man is ashamed of such a lengthy and important time in his life, then he is bloody well close to admitting his failure as a person. More than failure, his ineptitude, his hopelessness, his inadequacy."

A flood of tears fills his red eyes, and I am embarrassed. One is always embarrassed at such open suffering. If you are watching it in the distance, you can laugh. You can say poor man and you can laugh. And if you are close enough to the person, you can reconcile the pain and you can comfort. But if you are the sole audience and if you are just an acquaintance, you can only think and cover your embarrassment with silence.

"But I am ashamed and I am ashamed not of the conditions, not of the outward realities. I am ashamed of my personal reactions, my singular and narrow response.

"I have never let myself love. To be sure, there were times of excitement. A quick intake of perfume. I liked but I never loved. I never wanted to let go. I was afraid and I knew that, but it didn't matter. I would consciously stop myself. I would take the grace of passion and I would cut it in two. I would smother it with reason. I would pick it apart. I have been very safe, and I have missed it all."

I too feel that, have experienced it, regret it. Not that I have never loved. But in my loving I have sought apocalypse; and when I didn't find it, I blew it. I want to talk to him about my dead marriage, but I cannot. I cannot explain that I was given magic, only to lose it and never trust it again, but to long for it.

"I took an easy way out when I married. I had the opportunity and I said the hell with love. But you cannot live so closely with a maid. I could have let myself love her, but I hated her instead. I was bloody happy when she died. The crap we do in the name of safety."

Or in the name of greed. What does one do if one can be satisfied with nothing less than everything?

"Sometimes I wish I could go back. I'd walk the Liverpool streets in the afternoon. I'd fill my lungs with the smell of the morning rain. Do you know how fresh the human breath feels when it is cold outside, another breath close to yours? I'd smell flesh and I'd cling to it."

But we cannot go back, that is the irrevocable fact. We look to the future and we look to the past, but we are forever fixed between the two and that is where we must fulfill ourselves or not. I can return to my first bit of sex no more than I can remember my second. I must taste the present, and that is my problem. I have forever dreamed myself out of it.

"One day I told my father that I wanted to leave Liverpool. He said something that I remember a lot. He told me that when I left I should take it with me. But I didn't understand what he meant until it was many years too late."

"Ah, shh-it, Red. I know how you feel, but don't get all pissed off about it. I mean, a nigger's a nigger, but this is their country. Gotta be someplace where a coon can act natural. Let the little shit be that way, long's he doesn't come on with no smart ass."

"He *is* smart ass. All the time, 'Here's my handwork, here's my handwork.' That shit-eatin' smile. Bastard makes me mad, makes me lose my appetite."

"Ah, shh-it, Red, shh-it."

At the Green Virgin Club on a weekday night. You are sitting with some diggers you know from the club, one Englishman at the table. Someone makes a bitter remark about the prostitutes who will not let you drink in peace, about the high-life band which seems much too loud. You agree. It is a blank day. Everyone gives it the same name. In retrospect it will be lost in the shuffle of events, buried by more significant moods, by thoughts. But you don't feel that at the time; instead the blankness, a belief that nothing is happening.

The full, dull force of the dry season hit the delta. There were no harmattan winds and there was no coolness at night. It had started in January and it peaked in March. The days were very bright and very hot. You had to shade your eyes from the yellow-white glare, from the heat that reflected upward from the paved streets, the snow-white sun sheet of the sandy soil. It was cooler at sea or in the bush, but the towns baked. At the end of the day, you found yourself exhausted from the sweat, drained and deflated, a salty burn in your eyes. But even then there was no relief. You could not sit in a chair and relax. In the morning your pillow was wet.

My apartment became unbearable. I had a small fan and I sat in front of it for hours, my shirt off, a handkerchief in my hand. I could not escape feeling like a trapped rat in an oven. The plaster walls held the heat. The tin roof intensified it. I stood on the balcony, longing for breeze. I looked up the street. The native activity had only slowed, but was still hectic. The different colors of dress and buildings seemed sharper, more distinct and pure. If all motion stopped, it would have seemed pastoral, the sun-washed postcard picture of the tropics. But my own discomfort sucked my attention away from this scene, and the motion of the scene itself destroyed what feeling of the pastoral remained.

There was a touch of madness about that motion. Market women and children lined the road. Truck pushers heaved and cursed with their loads. Taxis scrambled around pedestrians at top speed, honking wildly, their drivers sweating and screaming and chewing on cola nuts. The whole throng along the street a squirming, chattering, boiling mob. Tempers flared. Shopkeepers were assaulted. Incessant noise of music and voice. And I realized something I suspected from the first, accepted and even welcomed from the first—Nigerian society was indeed infected with a touch of madness, thinly veiled, now bubbling on the surface of all routine activity.

I frequently attended the club during this period. Its high ceilings and overhead fans dissolved some of the heat. The feeling of moisture came in from the river. It was very nice to sit in a straw chair at a marble-topped table, to sip a Chapmans, to hear the crisp, chilling tones of the British, even to experience, against your better moral judgment, a degree of the fading colonial sense of empire, of expatriation and exile, of the white man in white shirt and shorts, his shaded little gin world carved in a corner of the jungle.

It was at the club that I met the Hiblers. He was an American engineer, more refined than most of the others, closer to a businessman than a laborer. I had often seen his wife in the afternoons. She brought her small children to the pool, sitting sometimes poolside, sometimes with other wives, sometimes alone. He worked a week on, week off shift at Escravoes and was only with her half of the time.

There was something peculiarly American and attractive

about the wife. She was slender, perhaps thirty, tall, with an ample figure, soft, very soft blue eyes, and dirty blond hair cut very short, shorter in fact than my own. This gave her a pixie, girlish air. But she wore short, tight shorts or snug men's blue-jeans, and when you looked at her from the waist down, there was nothing pixielike about her. Her obvious attributes in this area made you reevaluate the hidden breasts and the girlish face. Some fundamental paradox would not go away, a faintly disturbing mixture of the innocent and the worldly. On second thought the pixie impression retreated altogether. And the blue eyes and the short hair, which earlier made you think of girlish-ness and freshness, made you think of decadence. Bitchery. Aggressiveness. Because her face was deceptive, and seeing this, you saw also that the deception was planned—and this notion of girl who was really woman but could still play girl teased you, made you think of the kind of dynamite experience that hits you the hardest in adolescence, when you find out that the certain something which appeals to you the most can often be the toughest, the trampiest, the most versatile and jaded.

Did you ever dream about a sexy little girl when you were fifteen? Did you feel humble, sweet? And did it ever turn out, after you had attributed "niceness" to her, this being part of your humility, the thing that kept you on the distant string— well, did it ever turn out that she later screwed seven or eight of the crudest guys at school? That type of thing.

I had been watching her a bit too openly, and I was sure she noticed it. It was because of this that I was a little nervous when she and her husband and another couple took the table next to mine. They were in loud spirits, and I was getting ready to leave when they invited me to join them.

For a long time I sat more or less silently, a little bored by their conversation. The women did most of the talking and most of it was of no consequence. The price of eggs, the problems of instructing a Nigerian cook, the snake they'd seen on the road. Both husbands were heavy-set, impassive men. They did not seem stupid, but solidly square. They took a modest interest in the talk, seemed very content with what they heard, and occasionally checked their watches and yawned.

Sometime during the course of the afternoon I became less silent, until I found myself dominating the talk. But it was not as if I were directing any real communication or engaging in any real dialogue. It was instead a self-centered monologue—a running commentary on my past life, interests, misadventures.

This type of performance was something I had often done before. It was an emotional thing—a torrent of words that swelled inside me, bursting free at odd intervals during the course of a month or a year. The habit came, I supposed, from being alone, from being apart from domestic bonds and the routine, petty way of life that sometimes results, the kind of routine that drains one's thoughts, waters one's language in the mishmash of daily trivialities. Nothing seemed more deadening and more dangerous to me than patterns of thought and speech which failed to drive, failed to probe into the more demanding concepts of life, failed to get beyond that chitchat rhythm of status quo, of female gossip that blinds the participant and barely covers a predominant moral vacuum underneath.

These people seemed that way, and it was their shallowness that made me pick up the slack. I did not always react like this. More frequently, perhaps, I began hating such people, becoming all the more silent. I think it was the wife that made me respond in this alternative, more accepting manner. In retrospect, everything I said that afternoon was in the nature of an act for her benefit. All my detailed, heart-opening rhetoric about the sea and my travels in life seemed bent toward that end, toward thrusting my personality through to her.

The thing is, when I am exploding in this way, I do not really care what impression I am making. I expose myself so completely that I must often appear a madman, some outrageous vagabond from the darker side of security. But in most of these instances, taking the floor has been its own reward; and if the people later seem to give each other knowing side glances when I am around, I am not particularly concerned. Occasionally I have made lasting friends in such a way, but more frequently I am later kept at arm's length and never again allowed into quite the same speaking position, and all of this is okay. In these verbal flurries I project my identity, and it is this projection rather than any planned reception that makes me do it.

On the other hand, I sometimes wonder to what extent I am deluding myself. I'm not averse to being well received and I've frequently noticed that I really seem to be engaging in a vicarious, impossible kind of seduction. In my conversation with the Hiblers, I was appealing to the wife. This was usually the case, and it shot the whole rationalization that I was talking for its own sake.

Sometimes the thought of adultery seriously passes across my mind. Then I find myself thinking how nice it would be, and from there it is but a short step to speculating about the wife's own inner systems and the probability of it ever happening— plotting, in fact, for a way to make it happen.

Diane quickly led me to the probability stage. I had to force myself to move my eyes around the table. My insides twisted as I sensed a willingness on her part. Her husband sat firmly, a polished kind of rock, ignorant of the underdealings of life. A problem of logistics, that was all it was, and that was why I found myself thinking that it would really happen, that it would not die in my imagination, not be the pipe dream of a foolish and offensive man.

Blunt lust. Each time I met her blue eyes, I thought it. I appraised, animally, that fair, mildly tanned flesh and I thought it. I took in that blond boy-cut leather-boot haircut and it excited me. And I said to myself, even as I was talking: Diane Hibler, I'm going to screw screw screw you.

I stood on deck and watched Pius bring his gear on board. The whole thing had come to a head about a week before when I was talking to Simpson in the galley. It was in the afternoon and we were out to sea. He played solitaire while I sipped a cup of soup.

"The soup," he said. "Too much onion. I always do it that way, too much or too little."

"It's not bad."

"Now you take your professional cook. He's got all these seasonings up here." He thumped his temple with his forefinger. "Yessir, right up here. Take a dish and he'll tell you exactly how much it needs."

"I talked to the office about it yesterday," I said. "Nobody on the list. They told me to go ahead and hire somebody myself if I wanted."

"It's not the food itself, not that. Anyone can boil some meat or throw some potatoes in the pan. It's the seasoning, cap. That's what it is."

"I'll have to get somebody. That torch guy's been by a couple of times. We might try him."

"Why don't you, cap. He wants the job, been by here when you were ashore even. Hell, we need a cook. We got little enough out here on this ocean as it is. We need some square meals."

"I'll talk to him in Escravoes."

"Can't be too soon," he said. "I was readin' one of them spy stories last night and this old boy was fixin' up a meal for this broad—made my stomach growl."

So Pius quit his job at the base and came on board. He bubbled over ecstatically when I hired him. It was a gift from the gods, another step in his personal climb to fame and fortune in America.

When he had his gear on board, I went down to the crew's quarters to see that he was settled in okay. They had cramped quarters in one large cabin, and I imagined he had had better facilities ashore, but he didn't seem to mind. He gave me a very professional look. "I'll be on duty in a matter of minutes. You will be surprised at my handwork. I can cook-o."

I went back on deck thinking about all this. It occurred to me that I felt a little intimidated by him now that he was on board. His staring at the torch had puzzled me, and this curiosity was even more aroused by the buoyant optimism of his dockside visits. But now I sensed a feeling of intimacy on his part that made me wonder how we'd get along in a more businesslike setting.

Not that I was all that high and mighty with the crew. I supposed they got better treatment from me than from the other Americans, and once or twice when we were in port I'd brought some beer on board and taken it down to their quarters, where we'd finished it together; but the fact was that I could not feel casual with anyone under my command. This eccentricity is what bothered me now about Pius. I felt that he was assuming too much, or assuming a relationship to which I could not react in kind. For one thing I could hardly be brotherly with only one member of the crew. They'd resent that even if they wouldn't necessarily jump to the conclusion that Pius was the proverbial "captain's boy." Perhaps it was less a professional matter than a personal one. Even with my closest friends I had always been reluctant to give up too much of my aloofness and independence. Not that I wasn't able to be close to people —rather that I could never simply share and share alike very easily. I held fast to a corner of privacy which no one could ever know, and Pius seemed much too quick in his questions about America and, in his manner, totally oblivious to any concept of privacy.

So I suddenly wondered about this, found myself worrying about it. Other things struck me too. I could imagine myself going ashore with Pius on my tail, friends on leave. As much as I hated the expatriate enclave, I could appreciate the social fix

I'd put myself in by taking Pius to the club or the other expatriate places around Warri. The Texans had no kind words for that —something worse than fraternizing was fraternizing with Nigerians. Even Simpson would lift an eyebrow. It is one thing to reject social pressure and ignore blunt prejudice, but it is quite another to have the guts to flaunt it altogether. I already felt caught in a cultural crossfire, hating the expatriate but needing him, and I wasn't sure how far I could really let myself go.

These thoughts ran across the top of my mind rapidly, and I was a bit ashamed of them. But my months in Nigeria and the racking sun had taken the steam out of my initial attitude. I wanted to reject my past, find a personal refuge in this corner of the world—yet I was an expatriate, not an immigrant. That was the only status I felt ready to accept, and I worried about destroying those few chains that bound me to it. It was contradictory, for I had fled to Nigeria as much a refugee as anything else. The only trouble with that is that nobody in his right mind wants to be a refugee.

Pius kept busy during those first days learning his way around the ship. His boast about his cooking proved to be no exaggeration and he was rapidly buttoning down his duties in a routine, effortless exercise with an efficiency that frightened the other Nigerians. Each day he polished and trimmed this exercise, sacrificing no quality in the process; and as he did, he had more and more time to hang at my heels and speculate about his next step forward. He wandered freely about the ship, visiting my cabin or the bridge with a boldness that shook up all sense of propriety among the others. He questioned me continuously about America, mixing this with cheerful hints of the varieties and depths of Nigerian life that he would introduce me to ashore. His every word and action seemed a calculated game plan, all appearing to proceed as scheduled, with no hint that anything might go wrong. The only time he seemed like his mysterious self, the one who watched the torch, was at night. He often stood alone on deck for an hour or two, facing the sea;

and I still wondered what fantastic dreams, as yet unspoken, fueled his designing mind.

But the others did not appreciate this trait. Even Simpson began to dislike him. "You know, cap, that new cook of ours is a regular con man. Wouldn't trust him if I were you. Spooky, I tell you. He's got all kinds of schemes going in and out of his mind. Always trying to get in real close."

"He does his job okay."

"Okay? Okay isn't the word for it. He does it like a machine. That boy's got a brain, cap, and I don't trust him."

I let it drop at that, but I did not like the way sentiments were building. I thought I sensed a growing resentment among the crew, and I wondered how all of this had managed to come about so suddenly. I thought about talking to Pius, trying to get him to slack off a little, fit more in the groove with the other crew members; but he seemed so cheerful and confident, so honest, that I could not bring myself to put the idea across. One night I did manage to ask him how he was getting along with his cabinmates.

He giggled lightly. "Oh, them. They are all different tribes. I am an Ibo. We are too different." He grinned and dropped the matter, as if his association with the others was something totally unimportant.

My mind toyed with this attitude, and I realized his carelessness. But what really plagued me was the discovery that he was more inscrutable than he seemed. Was he naïve to the harshness of life and the consequences of his actions, or was he indeed a con man? I found myself doubting him, becoming skeptical of his friendly advances.

I say I was plagued by these thoughts, but that is too harsh a word. They troubled me some, but they were more accurately only fleeting irritations. I soon accepted the situation and let it rest. There was nothing I could do about it really and I allowed Pius to go on with his intimacy toward me and aloofness from the others. I was never sure exactly what they made of the relationship, but I was damned if I was going to call him down for being efficient and friendly, albeit ambitious.

Diane Hibler did not fade away, nor did much materialize for a while. I saw her infrequently at the club. The heat knocked the resiliency out of me; but those final, sweltering days of the dry season were not without a sensation of enthusiasm. My life was becoming increasingly complex, a crescendo of social contacts multiplying and simplistic ideas leading to labyrinthine patterns in which nothing was simple. All components worked together to ease me out of my withdrawal. Perkins, who had accidentally stumbled across my path; Pius, who pushed himself into the middle of it—and her, whom I thought about and anticipated.

That anticipation generated an excitement of its own. Nothing needed to happen yet, because I knew it was coming. A serendipity about the timing. I could not alter it or control it. It altered me instead. I spoke to her briefly from time to time, to say hello, a banal comment or two, all the time waiting, watching that tough ass and waiting.

From the club to Ijoto and back again. Was there a better way to spend time? If so, it did not occur to me. Late at night, in my apartment, I smoked Indian hemp. The sweet honey smoke absorbed me. The gentle sensation of pleasure, beauty. It was somehow like sex itself—ohs as the drug caressed my lungs. Amusing wheels in the mind that seemed to sprout from nowhere. A sensuous relaxation. For some reason also I began taking Dexedrine, a pill or two whenever the mood hit me. I could feel my body twinging as it rushed through me. I was virtually gluttonizing myself with these drugs, and that satiation became a beauty in itself.

There was time for all of this, and time again for straight days at the club.

"It's simply horrid, Elizabeth. They say thirty thousand people were massacred in the North."

"Civil war, that's what it looks like to me. Roger heard something on the newscast this morning. There he is now. Roger, Roger, what was that the BBC said about the massacres?"

Roger pulls a mustache. "Quite outrageous, you know. The soldiers had gathered the Ibo refugees at the Kano airport. Then they machine-gunned them all."

"Oh, it was all over the North, Elizabeth. They went house to house through the Ibo quarters. And the civilians came through when the soldiers were finished and cleaned up the leftovers."

"The East is sure to secede."

"It's inescapable, my dear. Just a question of time."

And there were sailor nights too—orgies of drink and the streets of Warri. High life in the night. Pimps and prostitutes and talking drums. Texans. Big Red and others.

"That's right, hoss. I'm from Texas and I'm drunk. We read the Bible in Texas. Did you know that, boy? And I'm gonna give you a little freedom talk. Because I pulled myself up by my bootstraps, hoss, and I ain't got no respect for no man that don't do the same. The Lord put us on this earth to work, and Jesus Christ if there ain't nothin' I hate more than a sorry hand or a nigger. 'Cause I'm from Texas and I'm American. You got that, hoss?"

Mystery in those Warri streets. Somehow the days zip by in the dust clouds of taxis and motorbikes. And the noise of the night absorbs the chaos.

Perkins hunched over a plate of steak and eggs at the club. "Isn't it all rather preposterous, your coming out here like this? Even in the old days this was no place for settlers. East Africa was our spiritual home, but this? White man's grave, they used to call it. No place at all for a gentleman, no good for sundowners even. Too much red clay, dust, sand. Too much malaria, too much heat, too much noise and stink. Who do you think you're kidding?"

"Who were you kidding?"

"Yes, but my mistakes were possible. No one really knew how dead the old world was then. The past blinded us. But now there is no past. And anyway, it's too late for me, was too late then even. But I was honest with myself, my ignorance was honest. The writing may have been on the wall, but it wasn't big enough yet, one could still get by without noticing it. You should know better. This is nothing but a gigantic charade, what you're doing here. It might be well and good for a disgruntled man in America to look at a map and say Africa, I will leave this miserable technological hole and go to Africa. There in some primeval forest I will regain purity and live forever in peace."

"Yes, it was like that, something like that."

"Hogwash. A person like you, well traveled, an immigrant to Nigeria? In a day and age when immigration is fast becoming useless and obsolete? Sheer poppycock."

"You forget that my position isn't quite as placebound as yours, or anyone else's."

"Oh yes, yes, of course. You have your vessel. You a seaman, and you call it a boat."

"Expediency, it's the language of the day."

"But precisely what is that overgrown tug of yours? You call it a boat, you call it a ship, you sign your letters captain of the vessel such and such."

"Boat? Ship? What's the difference? She's at home on river and ocean alike, so she's both."

"So now it's a she. In my day something was one or the other."

I light a thin cigar I have been saving for an idle moment. I am much amused at his boiling, categorical twist of mind. "She's both. It's a ship, but I'd feel pretty ridiculous using the word 'ship' for what is more functionally a boat. The distinction doesn't matter anymore anyway. Complexity values other things more highly."

"What things?"

"I don't know. The moment, I suppose. That truth."

One morning Pius buttonholed me on the bridge. "Hey, boss, when do we reach Escravoes?"

A Nigerian quartermaster was at the wheel and Simpson was lounging on my bunk. The abruptness of his entrance and the question shot silence across the room.

"Two, three hours."

"Good." He beamed happily. "Tonight I will show you my house. My wife will fix us African chop."

The silence seemed even deeper. The quartermaster stared rigidly ahead, and I felt Simpson's gaze bearing down on me. Pius was violating all protocol between captain and crew, and I felt the blush of embarrassment rush over my face. I was irritated, not so much at his action as at the position he placed me in and had been placing me in since he came on board. I cut him off. "Talk to me later. I'm busy now."

He gave me a quick puzzled look and left. Almost as soon as he did, I felt guilty and later I found him in the galley. He was washing dishes and barely looked up as I came in.

"I didn't know you had a wife," I said.

He did not look at me but went on about his work. "Yes, boss, I've been married two years."

I leaned against the counter and lit a cigarette. "Is she a good cook?"

This got through to him and the quickness with which he changed was startling. The smile returned to his face, and he let a dish slip into the sink.

"Cook? Na-wha!" He kissed his fingertips delightedly. "She can prepare the best stew in Escravoes. When you taste it, you will see why she is my wife."

I accepted his invitation then and everything was back to normal. I had never been in a Nigerian home, and it would be a good experience. Still, in the back of my mind I worried about the violation of propriety. For all of my professed individuality, I could not get away from this. I wondered if any social standards of the native or the expatriate were really being violated at all; or if it sprang from my own mind, dredged up from some dark area of prejudice that I would not admit for what it was. I began to doubt where I really stood on anything.

Once away from the boat and the confining sense of role that I felt on board, I was better able to respond to Pius in kind. His home was in the village, just behind the main street, and not fifty yards from the Mexico Bar. It was made of mud, packed firmly so that it was as hard as stone and smoothed on the surface like cement. The roof was tin. Wooden door and wooden window frames were set in, much as they would be on any other kind of structure. I had seen hundreds of such houses; but now that I was a guest in one, I examined it in detail.

The inside was very neat, with straw matting on the floor. The walls were painted blue and there were curtains at the windows. It was hardly a mud hut at all, but a tight, attractive dwelling, naturally insulated from the heat outside, more attractive and suitable, in fact, than dozens of urban apartments I had seen in America, more comfortable than cheap three-dollar hotel rooms I had often slept in, more sanitary than acres of rat-infested slums that littered my own country. A small wooden table sat in the center of the room surrounded by four peculiarly African chairs—wooden, but low-slung like easy chairs with large, soft cushions.

His wife was more than attractive. I hadn't expected a market mammy, but I was surprised at her beauty. She wore a white western blouse with a long, tight, ankle-length skirt made from bright-blue native cloth. It fit much as an evening dress, snug around her buttocks and thighs. Her eyes were big and liquid, but not nervous like many Nigerian women's. Instead they rested confidently on you with just a hint of amusement. She was very young, not more than eighteen or nineteen.

After a short bow she was out of the room. Pius called a small boy from next door and sent him for beer. He offered me also a cigarette and a small chunk of cola nut.

"Chew it," he said. "It is part of our ceremony for guests. I have already broken it."

I took a small bit and chewed it cautiously. The nut was very bitter and dry and it constricted the skin around your gums. It was a stimulant, and I had often seen taxi drivers chew it to keep them alert.

"There is a long ceremony for the cola," he said. "It is very formal and many of us have discarded it. Usually the nut will be inspected by the guests, that is before it is broken. Some words are said and the eldest will break it. Then all inspect the breaking and the eldest will eat first."

"What is its meaning?"

He shrugged and grinned. "No meaning. It kills time. Most customs are only for killing time. In the modern age we do not have so much time to waste."

"The modern age is too full of hurry," I said.

He grinned again. "But how can you say that, boss? You are an American."

"America isn't all roses."

"I don't understand."

"Not everything in America is good."

He laughed, not believing that I was serious. "You feel the heat in this house? It makes your clothing stick?"

"Yes."

"In America we would have an air conditioning."

"Maybe."

"And air conditioning is good, boss. If I had money, I would buy one."

He beamed victoriously, but I would not allow him the point. "People have lived a long time without it."

"Of course, but the past is darkness. There was too much suffering."

"Isn't there suffering now?"

He laughed again. "Yes, boss, that is what I am saying. But now there are places where you can suffer with air conditioning, and it is better to suffer with air conditioning than to suffer without air conditioning."

His wife soon brought in the food and set it on the small table in front of us. She did not eat with us, but privately, outside by the kitchen. The meal consisted of pounded yam and egusi stew with meat. You took a piece of the yam in your fingers and flattened it into a scoop. It was doughlike and did this easily. Then you scooped up some of the stew and put both together in your mouth. The stew was heavily spiced, and until I got used to it I had to go slowly, taking more yam than stew.

Pius noticed my streaming eyes. "Is the pepper too much?"

"It's okay."

"There is not as much as usual. It is the pepper that makes the taste."

As much as I could tell, with the intense burning in my mouth and throat, the taste was very rich, and it irritated me that I could not eat faster.

"You do not have this kind of chop in America?"

"No."

"But the American black men, do they not have native foods?"

"Yes, but it's not like this."

He put a huge dipped chunk of yam in his mouth and swallowed it without chewing. "I will miss it there," he said. "European chop is not enough for me. Only hamburgers, they are good. Do you know hamburgers?"

"Hamburgers?"

"Yes, boss. They are wonderful."

I sweated from the pepper for a time when we were finished, but I liked the food and it felt good when it was full in your stomach. "I like your chop," I said.

"Yes," he agreed. "There are so many things in the stew. Only a woman can prepare it."

We sat quietly for a while and he showed me a collection of photographs which he kept in a small cardboard box. Most were of people, and he identified them for me, explaining the extent to which he knew them and what they were doing now.

When we had seen them all, he came back to a picture of a girl in western dress lounging on a sofa. "I want you to know this girl," he said.

"Let's visit her sometime."

"I told her we would come tonight."

And so we wound through back streets until we came to the compound where she stayed. Pius left us alone after a few minutes and it was awkward because I didn't know how to make conversation with her. But she did not seem bothered by the silence. We got along all right without talking.

Friday night, five o'clock—library hour at the club. A corridor-like alcove between the billiard room and the bar. Glass-paneled doors opening to the pool. Wooden panels sliding back to reveal the books. A good library, remnant of an earlier, more literate expatriate population.

Library. You know it has started when Bertha arrives with her husband. She is a big cockney and her husband usually waits at the bar while she picks two or three books. She joins him back at the bar while the barman pours her a drink, and in a very short time her bellowing, nonstop laughter fills the room. It is a contagious signal, indicating that, library formalities completed, it is time to get down to the serious business of weekend sundowning.

Everyone packs the club for library. Petroleum wives with scrubbed children. Dirty, T-shirted riggers, just back from the fields. Crisp British clerks in cool white shirts. A table or two of sailors. A sprinkling of faces who appear only for this occasion. They sprawl around the pool, pack around the bar, set tables together and chatter insistently. A few get books, but most are on their third or fourth drink. The stewards serve hot potato pies with mustard. Someone has spilled a mug of beer. Mama, mama, Harold splashed me. What you readin', hoss? Two Chapmans. Sit down, Ray, sit down for God's sake. Drink. Drink. Stumble. Spill. Laughter, God almighty. Cheers, hoss. Conversation to a roar. Because it's LIBRARY LIBRARY LIBRARY.

Diane drunk at my table without a husband in sight. A round of Irish sailors pumping her for the tab. One lone Texan who does not like what is happening and soon drifts away. Her voice squeals, pants, cuddles, self-satisfied. "Don't you have a first name?"

"People just call me Christopher."

A quick, careless touch of her hand to my knee. "I'll get used to it." Her legs crossed tightly over her crotch, a smug, secret little twinge of pleasure as she squirms, wiggles her butt into the chair.

Steward at her elbow. "Mam?"

"Of course, I've got it here." Fishes in her purse for a five-pound note.

"Me mother used to read a bit."

"Na-wha-wha-wha."

"I don't see your husband much."

"Ahh!" A wave of the hand. "I'm alone every other week."

"Time to read—me mother would say that."

"You feel alone in this country."

"Do people call you Chris? Drop by and see me sometime for a drink." Fishes in purse. Pencil, paper, writes address.

"When?"

"He'll be home next week. Sometime the week after. Any morning."

Initial surge breaking up now. Red sunset dying. People thinning out. Stumbling off to dinner. Last chorus of laughter from Bertha.

"I'm cold, Mama."

"You're dripping water."

"Cold, Mama."

"Let's go. Come on, let's go home and change."

"Be seeing you."

"Don't forget the drink. Anytime. In the morning."

"Be seeing you."

"Be seeing you."

"Cheers."

Sliding the panels back over the books. Cigarette butts and beer. No more pies. Stewards mopping up. Be seeing you. LIBRARY LIBRARY LIBRARY.

I woke up with a start. It was a foggy-hot morning, reliable signal for the long, hot day. I got up quickly, splashed water on my face, and made my way to the bridge.

We were already unloading, tied up to the rig. The quartermaster had brought us alongside. Simpson lounged at the map board. "How long we been in?" I asked.

"Half hour, hour, not long."

"Any radio?"

"No."

"I'm going aboard."

I could not have waited longer. Anxiety pumped in my limbs. I tightened my belt and retied my shoes and went down on deck and onto the ladder and up to the deck of the rig. The crane was almost overhead and I had to watch it. One of the men looked at me, wondering what I was doing. I went on over to the work shack. The foreman was new to me.

"You the captain?"

I introduced myself.

"We'll have you on your way in a couple hours."

Blood really pumping now. "I'd like to see Red. Is he on duty?"

"Red? Oh, shh-it no. Probably hung up by now. He took a chopper into Escravoes last night. His week off."

Blood still pumping, doesn't stop for a moment or two. Is it relief or disappointment? Then it will have to be in Escravoes. Better that way.

A Speculative Look at Pius

He was a city boy and this distinguished him to some small extent from the great mass of Nigerians who lived in cities but still had a village somewhere that was home. The city was Enugu; and if there were those who thought of this place as being too clean, too artificial, too much a product of colonialism to be truly Nigerian, there were others, like Pius, who thought of it as the Nigeria of the future.

Even as a child he had little sense of the past. He was an Ibo tribesman, and his sense of identity was basically tribal, but he rejected the cultural trappings of tribalism. He dismissed traditional life with hardly a thought. It was the future that mattered, not the bush. And like Enugu, he sought the future in a western mold. It was as if nothing was really native, as if the word "native" had no meaning at all. Because it was all now, starting now and going forward. Building concrete blocks and embracing an industrial world that never looked back.

He was the youngest of eleven children; his father died while he was still quite small. He mourned the death dutifully, but the fact was his father had always seemed a distant kind of figure. His father's room had always been a place of mystery in the compound. He was always the master, not merely father in a physical sense, but psychological father of the compound itself. He seldom spoke except to give orders, and one responded to him with an awe that forbade a more egalitarian sense of blood.

Yet the father himself was a gentle enough man. He retired from the civil service and kept a small yam farm at the edge of town. At times he would take the boy to work in the field and he would explain the sweat and the sun that is farming. He told about earlier days, when all men farmed, when the yam harvest was an occasion that set the year more than the white man's calendar. He reminisced about life in the village, the intricate mysteries of juju and solid clay beneath your feet, and relaxed palm wine Sundays.

These things constituted only a fleeting imposition on the boy's mind. Stories of the village did not interest him. His interest was in another direction.

This rejection of father was not a rejection of family for its own sake; for his mother was always the guiding, nearly beatific figure in his life. It was she who raised him, who assigned him chores, who taught him respect for his father, and cemented a kind of relationship that westerners would think overprotective. The boy responded in kind, even through his adolescent years. His father had been an authority figure, but it was the mother who made the home. Constantly at work, she gave love, warmth. His respect for her increased, rather than dwindled, as he grew older. She was every inch the pidgin-speaking market mammy personality that Europeans find a bit disgusting. She was utterly lacking in feminine charm; but the boy accepted the hard-working, often cackling mammy as the best image of motherhood, and like all Nigerians, he zealously and unabashedly revered this institution.

She was a big woman, much larger than the father, and more complex than she appeared. Deep beneath the mammy stereotype lived a shrewd and efficient mind, an economic drive and practical sense that set the tone for the boy's ambitions. After the father died, while the boy was still in primary school, the mother sold the yam farm and invested in a small building company. It was more than an investment, for she virtually founded it. Starting with less than a hundred pounds, she hired a manager, bought sand, cement and a few rudimentary tools. Manual laborers were contracted on a day-to-day basis, and soon her first house was completed and sold. It was a small, square affair, like a mud hut, but with concrete walls beneath the tin roof. Laborers were cheap, grossly underpaid, in fact, and such business brought tremendous profits. The business expanded, a draftsman was hired for more complex structures, and she soon reaped in profits the father had never dreamed of. She owned her own compounds, collected rents, became known among Enugu's elite. She was overbearing and harsh with her servants, a *nouveau riche* with an automobile and driver, addressed as madam, a self-made aristocrat of the type respected by Ibo tribesmen more than any traditional upper-classman.

The boy was an alert but mediocre student, for his attention wandered, and more than many of his instructors he sensed the inadequacy of an educational curriculum imported from Britain. He attended a secondary trade school which emphasized draftsmanship and building.

He left school after completing only three years of this study, and surprisingly his mother accepted this decision. An obvious new factor was entering Nigerian life—Americans. Unlike the British, they had little use for formality. They were there for a simple reason which the boy well understood—they were there to make money. Oil brought them, and this industry stimulated other industries. The boy quickly saw that a small, primitive building contractor offered no competition to the white construction men with their equipment and materials and precise design. The mother's company might go on indefinitely building native compounds, but the really modern contracts—the banks and hotels and western-style stores—were being built by the foreign companies.

He worked for an Italian highway-building firm for a while, and having established an income, he married. He broke tradition to do so, for he went outside of his own tribe for a bride, picking an Itsekiri girl he had met through a co-worker across the Niger River, near Warri, where many Ibos, overpopulated on their own land, had moved. His own family did not object to the match, but there was a period of many long weeks of negotiation before the girl's father agreed to the union and accepted a bride price.

Pius had changed much in this time. A few of his friends kidded him with the nickname "California" for the adroitness with which he adopted western customs. He listened to the Voice of America jazz hour, he bought a guitar and imitated American folk music, he read countless magazines about the United States. He once got hold of an exposé article about Times Square in the early hours of the morning, and the complex interactions of prostitutes and thugs and homosexuals and heroin puzzled him, but secretly thrilled him. He could not understand such a place, but he quickly saw that this predatory world offered a challenge and an animal chance to get ahead which he wanted to see.

It was then that he became disillusioned with his trade, for the Italians kept the managerial positions for themselves and selected only a few Nigerians to operate the big equipment which did the work so quickly and efficiently. A new business was booming. The oilmen needed catering and they paid well for any young Nigerian who could wear a white coat and keep his mouth shut and carry drinks on a platter. He got a job as a steward in Escravoes, and then as a cook.

Pius saw nothing offensive in this role. Quite the contrary, it paid well and it brought him one step closer to America. As much as he disliked many Americans, he nonetheless clung to that country as a personal Mecca. He knew what he was about, and he readily accepted the game of role playing in order to get it.

five

THE RAINY SEASON came quickly. One day it was dry and hot, and the next day it was there. It wasn't steady rain at first, but short, bursting storms which became more frequent as time wore on. The sky would suddenly darken and the wind would whip the dust in the street. Then pedestrians scurried for cover. Cars sped to urgent destinations. Until the sky was black and the water pounded down. It beat the windowpanes and rattled like machine gun fire on tin roofs. The air became more humid and sticky than usual; but when the first burst of the downpour had subsided some, you could open the window and feel the clean-smelling rush of cool air flooding against your face. Down below, in the street, the water roared through the drainage ditches, ferrying away the accumulated garbage of the dry season. These rains would not have been bearable on a year-round basis; but ending the hot season as they did, they brought relief and needed variety.

I took a taxi to Diane's address. It had rained in the early morning and was sunny now, but in the distance it looked as if the rain would return. It was an old house, a big wooden house, but it was well built and attractive—a square, rambling affair of the kind that white men used to live in in old movies about Africa. The house was highlighted by a huge front porch, or veranda, with large wooden shutters which opened upward on hinges, propped open by wooden poles. It was set well back from the road, hedged in, with a huge lawn spotted with shrubbery and flowering trees. A small second-floor addition had been tacked onto the back of the structure. This destroyed some of the building's symmetry, but was small enough not to be noticed from the road. Small servants' quarters were built in the back, removed from the house, much as a garage. But approaching the house you noticed only the spreading porch, dominating the house as a testament to the days of the Union Jack and gin tonics for the heat.

We sat on the same porch and drank gin Chapmans, an old colonial drink, but there was no heat now, only the chaotic uncertainty of a rainy-season morning.

She mixed refills at a small sideboard to the back of the porch. Her housegirl was sweeping noisily inside the house. "I hate asking Patience to fix drinks this early," she said, "so I have this little bar out here where I can do it for myself."

I looked back inside but could not see the girl sweeping. "What does she think?"

"Patience? We don't pay her to think. Anyway, I'm the only one she talks to. A double this time?"

"All right. Where are the kids?"

"At the European school. They stay till one."

She finished with the drinks and came back to the chair next to mine. "Relax. Are you always so jumpy at this time of day?"

"I keep imagining husbands coming in."

She laughed and took a long swallow from her glass. "Don't worry about that. People have been here before. He never finds out."

She crossed her legs and looked at me and gave me a quick, sheepish smile. But for the moment she was more interested in the drink. She held it cupped in both of her palms, close to her lips, alternately sipping at it and raising it up for larger swallows. It held her attention much as the first cup of coffee holds one who has just awakened. She looked, in fact, as if that was what she had just done. Her face was full and rested, her short hair slightly ruffled. She was not yet dressed, but wore a flimsy white dressing gown, tied with a sash at the waist and open in front down to her breasts, showing their tops and the dark cleft between them. She was barefooted, but her feet were white and very clean, and when she propped them on the railing of the porch, the bottoms showed only a trace of dust from the floor. The extension of her legs brought the front of her gown well above her knees, her slender, tanned legs forcing themselves on my attention until I could not help looking at the very light, smooth blond growth of hair across them and the ample, firm flesh of her thighs.

She snuggled back in her chair. "I've heard them talking about you at the club."

"What do they say?"

"They say you spend too much time with the Nigerians, and something about an Englishman you hang around with."

"Perkins, I guess."

"One guy says you're unpatriotic."

"Unpatriotic?"

"You know, that you're not a good American, that kind of thing."

I let out a short laugh. "I came to Africa so I wouldn't have to be anything."

"Do you know a lot of them?"

"Who?"

"The Africans."

I shrugged. "My apartment is close to them. I know one of my crewmen pretty well."

"What's he like?"

"Okay. Pretty bright." I felt on the defensive. "He's aggressive as hell, but in a friendly way. He sort of forced himself on me."

She made a clicking, disapproving sound with her tongue. "They'll all do that if you give them half a chance. They're born politicians."

"I don't know. This guy's different. I mean, he does push and he is kind of a politician, but he's sincere too."

"I wouldn't be fooled."

I didn't want to press it so I let it rest and looked out over the yard. The sun had gone and it seemed certain to rain again now.

She offered me a cigarette and lit one herself. "What's all this talk about secession? Do you think there'll be a war?"

"There's already been fighting in the North."

"I know, but I can't keep up with the thing."

"I don't understand it all. It goes back to the first coup."

"It seems odd that all they say is really happening. It's so peaceful around here." She was silent for a moment, with a slightly disappointed look on her face. "I suppose it'll blow over."

"They say it's getting worse."

She gulped the rest of her drink and set her glass on the floor, then snuggled in her chair again. But she wasn't able to get comfortable and finally turned sideways, facing me, and resting her back against the arm. She slung her feet up onto my lap. I was a little startled and shifted in my chair, trying to look casual. One of her heels touched my genitals and I could not gaze naturally without dropping my eyes to her legs. I finished my own drink and set it on the floor.

"Are my feet dirty?"

I looked at them directly, as if for the first time, but did not notice dirt so much as the light-pink polish on her toes. "No, they're clean."

"Patience hadn't swept yet when I got up."

"There's some dust on the bottoms."

"Really?"

"Just a little."

She put out her cigarette. "I hate dirty feet. Will you brush it off?"

I put out my own cigarette and brushed at her foot, not too effectively. "I'm not expert at this."

"They won't bite you. Just sweep it off."

I took her foot fully in my hand then and brushed the bottom. The dirt would not brush off very easily and most of the dust wiped onto my hand. I brushed at it again, trying to get rid of the dirt, until it seemed that I was doing more caressing than cleaning. "Do you think they're pretty?" she asked.

"Your feet?"

"Well, yes."

"I've never been much at evaluating feet. But they're clean now at least."

She giggled. "Feet are cool."

I was still holding them, rubbing them a little, and I relaxed some and looked at her. I felt that little twinge that had first attracted me to her, that suggestion of little-girl innocence about her face—this freshness coupled with the air of casual decadence—and it was all I could do to keep my wits.

She cocked her head in my direction and gave me a teasing, shylike smile. "Let me see yours." She said it very offhandedly, but in a low, controlled voice that hinted at its deliberateness.

"What?"

"Your feet," she said.

"What do you mean?"

Again the little grin, half modest, half devil-may-care. Her lip quivered a little and for a quick, fleeting second I got the impression she was nervous, but the low voice was as level and deliberate as before. "Take off your shoes and let me see your feet."

I forced a laugh, suddenly embarrassed by the idea, or not so much at the idea itself perhaps—a play thing that you might do in teasing around, in a light mood, half as a joke—not so much

72

at this objective action as at the unexpected and underlying seriousness with which she gave the proposal. "You mean right here? Now?"

She tossed off all shyness and gave me a full smile, but a commanding, serious smile, a controlling manner and expression. "Sure."

"Won't it look funny?"

"Who will see? Come on."

I shrugged and grinned easily then as I gave in to her suggestion. When I had my shoes and socks off, she examined my feet gleefully, then placed hers back into my hands while I propped my own against the rail.

Her housegirl appeared at the door, and I automatically let her feet drop into my lap. The girl said that she wanted to go home.

Diane barely turned her head to acknowledge her servant. "All right, Patience. Be back at one o'clock. No later than one." Her voice had a peculiar shrill sound when she addressed the girl, a cutting whine, but hard as rock.

When the girl was gone, she jiggled her feet in my lap. "What happened? Are you embarrassed by her?"

"Just reflex."

"She won't think anything. Here." And she moved one of her feet up along the side of my face, poking at my ear with her toe.

Soon the wind began and light drops of rain were starting to fall, the gushing wind rattling the shades inside the house. She jumped up and I followed her around the porch slamming the shutters down, our bare feet flopping on the floor. It was almost dark with the shutters down and the rain began to fall heavily. We moved inside the house to a window where we watched the storm lash at the earth. The wind was still strong, not gusting now, but blowing steadily in one direction, unremittingly, like a gale wind, bending the tops of a row of palm trees. The rain made less sharp a sound on her wooden roof but it was still heavy and loud, thudding in a steady drone which seemed to isolate the house from the world outside.

She turned, very close to me, and faced me. The soft gown had shifted some and just barely covered her breasts. She let it hang, not bothering to draw it closer together. "Well?" she said. "Yes?"

"What are we waiting for?"

She moved her hands along my cheeks and around my head and pulled me to her. I put my arms around her and met her mouth fully with my own, both of us opening our lips together, moving into one another, her warm breasts against my chest. We ended a kiss, mouths still open, exploring each other's cheeks. I bit at her ear and slid my tongue inside it and moved my nose across her boyish hair. It was very soft and scented a little with the smell of powder or very light perfume. She slid her hands from my head, down my back, then under my arms, and down until they rested on my buttocks and she clasped me there. I moved my lips around, on and off her mouth again, then down her chin and neck and onto her chest. Her hands moved back to my head and pulled me down. I slipped to my knees— the front of her gown falling open all the way—and took her breast in my mouth, tonguing it, taking it as full into my mouth as I could, and out again, playing with the nipple between my lips.

"Come on," she said.

She pulled me up and led me upstairs to the bedroom in back. Neither of us spoke on the way up, not even when we were in the room and undressed and in the bed. She pulled the sheet up over my back and held my buttocks again, as I did hers, my mouth on her mouth and tongue on her tongue, as I entered her, plunged my prick inside her, in as far as it would go, she wrapping me, both of us flat against one another, twisting, fucking each other.

We lay together for a long while with the steady roar of the rainfall in the background. We did not talk much, and she did not seem interested in talking, preoccupied and aggressive as she was in her lovemaking. She did not lie still when we had finished but wrestled around beside me, tonguing and biting me on my arm and shoulder and chest. Her determined movements and the efficiency of her manipulations inhibited any real emotional feeling on my part, and something about the mechanical routine of how it all had happened gave me the same feeling that I had had with time-conscious prostitutes who methodically made love with the demeanor of a mechanic repairing an engine.

She did not stop moving around with her mouth, biting me around the neck and ears and cheek until she took my lower lip in her mouth and bit down hard on it. I let out a little grunt of pain and she released it. "Does that hurt?"

"Yes."

"Here, let me have your nose."

I half protested, but she took the tip of my nose between her teeth and bit down again. It hurt and I pushed her back. "Don't you like it?" she asked.

"It hurts too much."

"You won't die. Let me, come on."

She started to take it again but I turned my head. She turned it back with her hand. "Relax. Just relax and let me do it for a minute."

I let her take it again and she bit down on it and chewed for a moment, then released it and wiped the saliva off with her hand. "See, it's okay."

"I'll probably need plastic surgery."

She laughed and rolled over on top of me, and we screwed again like that, her pelvis twisting and grinding, as steadily and strongly as the rain outside, until I was shooting again, the stuff squirting out of me in violent spurts, as if my guts were rupturing loose with the pressure that pumped my seed into the moving, clinging box.

When we finished she kissed me gently around the eyes. "Do you love me?"

"I love you."

She jumped off and grabbed a box of Kleenexes, cleaning herself and lighting a cigarette at the same time. "It's getting late."

"What time is it?"

"After noon. You'll have to go."

She dressed slowly, drawing on her cigarette as she did. For some reason it felt good getting back into my clothes. I wondered how anyone could live with her and not die an early death. "What's your husband like?"

"You've seen him."

"He didn't say much."

She giggled, fluffing her hair at the mirror. "How could he? I have him trained."

"Trained?"

"Yeah." She took a last drag from her cigarette and put it out. "That's exactly it, trained. He goes to work and brings the money home. That's what I married him for. I keep him neat and out of trouble."

The sun was coming out again as I left, and it was like a new morning, a new day. But I was haunted by Diane, not only by the vision of her naked, writhing and clawing body against my own in the bed, but more strongly by her girlish face and boy-cut hair, the rabbitlike nervous movement of her head as she sipped at a drink or attacked cigarettes. I felt physically drained, but the image of the innocent-looking girl who was so proficient and mechanical in sex would not let me rest. I had little real feeling for her as a person, but an illogical, unsatiated craving kept her image—it was that, not what she really was, but the image her appearance conjured—fixed firmly in my thoughts, destroying other thought, refusing to leave. My appetite to know, to have and devour this image had not been satisfied. Instead the thrill of the image, the inescapable and elusive attraction of it, had increased. I had not had her. I was not satisfied. On the contrary, she had had me.

We were unloading at one of the smaller rigs when they brought the troops in. They weren't soldiers really, but bereted riot police, a crack Nigerian flying squad. We were just sitting alongside, and I was sipping some coffee on the bridge, when I saw the choppers, six of them. They set down on the rig, and the armed men poured out.

I had been only vaguely aware of the political troubles in Nigeria since I had arrived in the country; but in recent weeks the trouble had grown, dominating daily news and gossip, until here it was in front of me. The non-Ibo workers demanded that the Ibos go back to their native region, claiming that they were taking jobs away from local tribesmen. I hadn't heard about it before the police came, but evidently the confrontation stopped work, and violence threatened. The regional governor was strictly against tribalism and he sent the police in.

The troops stood on the platform and held the Ibo and non-Ibo workers together at gunpoint. They stayed on guard the whole time we were there, not even leaving the deck when a drenching squall crossed the area.

There was a strange, detached sensation in watching them. The closeness and the reality of the conflict struck me, but it still did not seem quite real. As close as I was to it, I was still removed, and I watched it from a distance. As if it were some play-action game or a television rehearsal. But it did make me wonder, for maybe the first time, wonder how I could legitimately claim this place as a place of exile when it threatened to explode in my face.

You have just gotten into port from an uneventful two weeks out and you take a taxi to your apartment and you sit down and ask yourself, "What now?" And you know it is another blank day. Still blank days when you thought they were over—that more agreeable experiences had vanquished them forever.

You still feel it that night when you go to a native movie

77

house. They are showing a third-rate Indian film, and the poverty of entertainment only rubs it in all the more. A Scotsman and his wife sit behind you and you meet them going out and head for the River Valley Hotel for a late sandwich. No excitement in this, and they comment on it. The blankness. All of you feel it, promote it as if there were never anything else, but you all choose to stay in the country. Any of you could leave tomorrow, and your talk makes it sound as if you might. But you stay.

The main market in Warri is a miniature city of its own—a walled commercial citadel, crisscrossing narrow lanes lined with stalls. It is a well-organized market so that one section or "block" sells kitchenware and another dry goods and so on for cloth and books and transistor radios and bicycles and almost anything else made on earth, with a separate, adjoining market for foodstuffs and meat. But when you step inside the outer wall from the street, this organization is not readily apparent; for the market teems with the noise and congestion of the buyers. Radios blare a hodgepodge of traditional and modern music, and hawkers beckon you in their direction. The stalls themselves seem overloaded with the wares they sell, so that pots and pans and brightly colored lengths of cloth invade the walking lanes, often hiding the stalls themselves, to the extent that one has the impression of threading through a jungle of merchandise and people all haphazardly crammed together.

That this old market, built long before the city's modern boom, was bursting at its seams was an obvious fact, for the main market area had spread well beyond the walls of the market itself, and this planned, designated center was only a part of the larger commercial heart of the city. Warri-Sapele Road, the highway which entered the city from the north, curved on through the business center as the city's main street and formed one boundary for the old market. Behind the market ran another prosperous street, Market Road. This was not as wide or well paved as Warri-Sapele Road, but just as congested. In some respects Market Road was a more colorful affair, for much of the traffic on the other main street was of a thoroughfare nature, concerned mainly with getting quickly through the area.

The pace on Market Road was hectic too, but the traffic here was more directly concerned with the shopping area itself. The road started along the river, by the native docks which handled passengers and cargo for the delta. It ran uphill from these docks, toward the market, lined all along the way with open-front shops of its own and frequent wooden stands of vegetables or fruit set closer to the edge of the street, curving past the market until it junctured with Warri-Sapele Road in an area of European shops—cold stores, clothing shops, appliance dealers, banks.

I liked the area—the noise, the congestion, the conglomeration of colors. One afternoon I was at the market buying curtain material for my apartment and was strolling up Market Road when it started to rain. I ducked under the tin, porchlike shelter in front of one of the shops. The rain came suddenly and pounded down as if it didn't intend to stop.

This was not unusual. As the rainy season swung along, the downpours became more frequent and longer, so that it rained regularly in the morning and again in the afternoon. It did not seem to drizzle much, almost always a quick, heavy rain which lasted a good hour or two and then stopped as suddenly as it started. The rains were too frequent to avoid getting caught. All you could do was take your chances, and wait if you were stranded somewhere.

I stood there ten or fifteen minutes, but wasn't able to get a taxi. Finally giving up, I dashed about half a block up the street to the Government Workers Club. This was a small, obscure bar next to one of the European supermarkets. It was an unpretentious place with wooden tables and huge, screenless windows. I had been there before with Perkins. They served beer and schnapps, and nobody seemed to know why they called it the Government Workers Club.

It was dark inside, with the rain roaring around it, and I had a large beer while I waited, more or less bored, near silence except for the storm. I was not alone in my waiting. There were two other customers, a white man and a Nigerian, neither of whom I'd seen before. I didn't join them in their conversation, but I could not help overhearing all they said. It was a long rain, and as it wore on, and as the drinking wore on, their talk became feverish and argumentative.

The white man was an American, in his early twenties, and on some kind of hitchhiking tour of Africa. He was a student, or part-time student, who had simply taken off with little more than a knapsack and a yen for "roughing it" across open country. I never learned how he bumped into the Nigerian, but bits of his background filtered through his talk. Politically he was very much an activist, and his disdain for American involvement in international affairs was his main preoccupation. He also seemed short of funds, and the possibility of finding temporary work with a European firm had brought him to Warri. But he did not seem inordinately anxious about this and hinted several times that his father in Cleveland had plenty of money if things really got tight. His dress was casual, but his clothes bore traces of the rugged kind of travel he'd been doing. He was the more aggressive talker of the two and irrevocably in love with his own ideas.

The Nigerian remained of a more mysterious mode. Neatly, nattily dressed in tight-fitting suit, white shirt and thin tie stylishly arched upward a little just below the knot, he made low comments in a careful British accent. He might have been a clerk or a civil servant or a barrister or whatever, but he was different from the Nigerians who worked for oil companies or waited on tables, different even from the mass of neighbors who crowded into the flats surrounding my building. He was genuinely Nigerian, make no mistake about that, just different from any Nigerian I had come in contact with.

He only glanced at me once or twice, but his expression made it clear that he knew what I was and that he had little use or interest in any expatriate—no fawning dependency like the stewards at the club, no casual amusement like the street boys and market mammies who yelled at you when you walked, no insatiable curiosity about the American myth, no adoration and desire to get to the States like Pius. His attitude was detached, proud, not hostile, but cold for a Nigerian; and his manner seemed to say that he was above all those others, no boy juggling for the white man's money or patronage, far removed from the existential materialism of the street, too knowing and mature to admire my country, too conscious of his own comprehension to get caught up in the innocent and simple dreams of progress so sacred to most of his fellow citizens—as if he had somehow by-passed, jumped ahead of all these cultural forces, was skeptical yet brooding on unfathomable dreams that were more sophisticated than those of the others and that he alone could understand.

Their most active conversation started when they got on to Nigerian politics. The American pushed the topic. "How can this country stay together when everyone thinks of his tribe first?"

"The same way it came together in the first place."

"How do you mean?"

"Artificially. If the law says it's one country, then that makes it one country." His speech was literate, cool.

"But you can't just bind people together with legal devices like that."

"Why not? What other way is there?"

The American seemed exasperated and he spoke rapidly. "With human feeling, a sense of community, something like that. People have to learn to feel together. Once they do that, the political systems will fall in line by themselves. You're trying to put the cart before the horse and it won't work. The government becomes a repressive force spending all its time keeping the lid on, enforcing unity where there isn't any."

The Nigerian was silent for a moment. He was not making idle talk, but carefully considering what the other had said. "You're partly right, I think. And if keeping the lid on becomes repression, becomes more repressive than even the most ideal government inevitably has to be, then the government's wrong. But I don't see a total sense of community as possible, not now or in a thousand years. Unless man becomes no more individualistic than an ant, and I don't think that's likely. I don't even think it's desirable."

"So the human race just goes on like it is, every man his own island struggling against everyone else, and cooperating only when the law forces him to."

"I didn't say that. I guess sometimes you'll be more together than other times, and that's what we have to do, move together like that. Maybe man will evolve until there's enough community to overwhelm the conflict, but who wants to go to the extreme, who wants everyone to be a carbon copy of the same thing, like a herd of cattle? Of course it could go the other direction. Or maybe we're already at the end. Maybe there won't be a future for us."

"That's what I'm saying. That's why we need the sense of community."

The other spread his hands in a gesture of futility. "But how do you get it unless you set up devices, laws, institutions to keep men in check?"

"Education; I don't know. But I don't know about institutions. They're repressive, whatever they're set up to do."

They paused again, and I sipped my drink. It was not the kind of conversation one often heard in Warri and it intrigued me, for I had thought about it many times but could never decide which side of the fence I stood on. I valued my individuality as much as my life and I had never submitted well to any institution, but I understood the sense of community too. I tended to agree that there would be no future without it.

"So what happens to Nigeria?" the American asked. "You just

force it to stay together? And what about the eight million Ibos? You hold them in check, and if they don't like being smothered in the rest of the country, you kill them."

"Take time, take time. It's easy for you to take their side; their ideas are closer to yours. But nobody's setting out to kill them or hold them in check. They started the trouble when they set themselves up as an elite, when they overthrew the civilian government and put the power in their own hands. Doubtless they have their reasons, but the rest of us have our own for saying that they can't dominate us and can't tear us apart, that they're already part of us, and the problems will have to be worked out within that framework."

The American made no reply and lit a cigarette, his face deep in thought. The Nigerian was as poised and relaxed as ever. He did not seem overly concerned about the conversation nor displeased with it. A calm kind of interest in the American, but nonchalant, non-urgent. There was a suggestion of mockery about his attitude, as if he were grappling with the ideas of a child, a foreigner who could not possibly understand his country or the inner space he inhabited. But this demeanor stopped short of being offensive; it remained too detached for that.

"What about your own country?" he asked. "You pass laws to make your people accept black children in your schools; is that bad? And you treat them like baggage when there isn't any law to stop you; is that good?"

"No, but that's another thing. America is already doomed."

"How would you change it?"

"I'd tear it up." Violence flashed in his eyes. "I'd close it down and tear it up, and take property away from those who have too much of it and use it only for themselves at the expense of everybody else. We have too many fat cats."

"Blood in the streets?"

"If it takes that. We have to get over the idea that people can do whatever they please in the name of individualism, and we have to get rid of the people who have too much."

"And what of your father's wealth? He apparently is able to subsidize your world travels, while other Americans are hungry. Him too?"

"I suppose. There can't be exceptions."

The Nigerian smiled slightly, neither approving nor disapproving. "You might well consider why the rest of the world shouldn't treat your entire country the same."

They trailed off into other subjects, but the conversation stuck with me. I agreed with much the American said, and certainly his bitterness toward the States was no more extreme than my own. But something about him did not seem right. The irony of a revolutionary who lived off the fruits of that which he opposed discredited his integrity. And I soon found myself feeling hatred toward him—not for his violent ideas, but for what he was, his father's son, who could have money sent from Cleveland, who could hide his own fat cat status beneath a knapsack and a hip interest in political theory. I could see his home, in a suburb perhaps, safely out of range of the ghettos and the misery in the heart of his own city, and I could see him in seminars, safely espousing revolution with other bright young men, contemptuous of those less gifted, each using and taking his inherited portfolio for granted.

I had not thought about it before, but I realized now that this American was my enemy as much as any other. I had left the States to get away from his father as much as I had left it to get away from any redneck. His intelligence, his concern and his revolutionary talk did not hide his underlying hypocrisy. And if American fat cats were to be rejected, then he was as fat as any of them, and nothing he could say or think would rectify what he materially was. I hated him.

Three weeks later, same setting: the Government Workers Club, musty, dark, quiet, pounding rain again outside. I am with Perkins and we are sitting by one of the big windows watching the flooded gutters beside the street. The barman wants to close the wooden shutters, but the rain is not blowing in and we keep him from doing so and enjoy the view from this dry refuge. We are drinking schnapps.

Perkins has slipped into his pose as Dutch uncle. "This is the apex, the back of the rainy season. It pours and pours. I've seen it go on like this for three and four days at a time, not even a pause, no moment of silence. You know why I like it?"

"Why?"

"Because it stops everything, exactly that. It comes out of the sky and it stops this city cold. We all dig in when it comes. We find a little hole, a nook or cranny somewhere, and we wait it out. It gives us a chance to be alone with ourselves, to examine our faces in the mirror while we wait out the rains. And it is good, this, because it's the only time for us here. Nigeria gives us no other chance. This is the only time one can be alone, can really feel alone."

We pause and I watch this rain that the old man talks about. He is right. It does stop everything. It hushes all the racket of native life and clears the swarming streets. Watching it you feel isolated. It hits you that you are in a foreign place, very far from home. The sandy soil becomes mudlike and all color seems vanquished. It is dismal, but not unattractive—because you feel that you are very near the jungle. It is like being in another time, some premodern age, removed from instant communications, the accessibility of rapid transportation. Alone with the mud and the rain and the sky and the trees. Sheltered from it, but watching it, patiently, dumbly, as an ape waits in his cave, secure but on guard, waiting for the sun. You feel very primitive, very anxious. You feel that you are at the end of the earth.

Perkins, belching his drink: "You're an odd one all right. Christopher the odd one. But you're getting along in time. It won't be long and you'll have been here a year. And still I don't know why you came."

"Like you. I came to live."

"Some life. What does it give you?"

I am tired of his pressing this subject, but he will not be placated. "What is there to have? A job, a home, sex, a friend, a Nigerian crewman who puzzles me, a glass of schnapps."

"All things you could have anywhere."

"Yes, but they're different here. It's different here, you know that yourself. I like it here. I like being away from the States."

"Different, that it is. But you'll go back. When you've got what you want, what you needed when you came, you'll go back. I won't, though. I can't. I'll never get back. Stuck here, virtually a sleepwalker, that's me."

Those were mainly months of contentment, and I lived at a more relaxed pace than I had in a long time. I did not feel stranded and I did not feel like going back, whatever Perkins said. Questions of why and where did not seem to matter then. All bitterness evaporated. The sense of urgency that I felt at first was gone. And the future did not seem to matter. There was a timeless quality, the magic that a schoolboy feels in the midst of a summer vacation. Inconsistencies about my immigration were no longer important, because I ignored them, unsettled as they were, let them rest in a nowhere land. Because everything was drifting, drifting along well without them. I did not want to come to grips with them for the moment. Instead I lived, freely, free, what people call free, a free man.

My acquaintanceship with Pius grew into a real friendship. He followed me about the ship and freely visited the bridge and my cabin, more like a guest than a crewman. The completeness of his casualness continued to alarm the rest of the crew until they came to regard him with open contempt. There was even a hint of censure toward me, but it wasn't extreme. They felt that I was being too soft, too naïve and good-natured in my attitude toward this upstart. The situation bothered me some, but not as much as it had at first, and I no longer felt self-conscious in my relationship with Pius. I only regretted that they saw something sinister in our friendship, convinced that he was taking advantage of me and that I was too weak or blind to put a stop to it.

But the friendship itself seemed harmless enough. Perhaps he *was* taking advantage of me to some extent, and at times I was still annoyed by his assumption that he did not have to worry about his status or performance as did the rest of the crew. At first I frequently suspected that he was consciously playing a game, deliberately imposing on me and quite aware of what it was he was doing. I did not know what had been in his mind when he first approached me, first forced himself on me, but I was sure that his behavior had since become automatic.

He still bombarded me with countless questions about America, and his optimism that he would somehow get there, that perhaps someday I would dig into that vast reserve of savings that all Americans were known to have and finance his way, and that once there he would soon be rubbing elbows with millionaires—this remained as strong as ever.

At night, when we were in the Sea of Steel, he still stared at the torch. I stepped out on deck one night and he was there, no longer pressed against a wire fence on a sandbar, an unknown dreamer in the darkness, but staring just as intently at the light as he had been then. We were on our way back to port, with no problems, the quartermaster at the helm, and I stepped over next to him. He noticed me but did not look away from the torch for a moment.

"It could burn like that for years," I said. "It depends how much gas there is."

"It was here when I first came to Escravoes."

"Why do you stare at it?"

"I don't know, boss. Something in it is good. I only watch it at night, when my handwork is finished. It is better than sitting in the cabin."

"The others are in the cabin. You could talk to them."

He grinned as if the idea were outlandish. "What do they

know, boss? Besides, I am the only Ibo. They are jealous of me."

We had discussed tribalism and the political trouble only in passing, but Pius did not seem to be alarmed by what was happening in the country. He waved the issue aside as something incidental, insignificant in comparison to his personal ambitions.

"What do the others say about the trouble?" I asked.

He grinned again, wider than before, taking it for a foolish question. "We do not talk."

Once again he turned to the torch, untroubled, confident. I wondered if he was as secure as he seemed. Hundreds of Ibos had left the region, and dozens of others were following suit every day. In Warri the motor park was busier than I had ever seen it, bursting with Ibos seeking bus transport to the East. They were afraid and they were taking all of their possessions with them—beds, mattresses, pots, bicycles—stacked on lorries and taxis. Patches of Warri were greatly depopulated, with closed storefronts where Ibo merchants had left.

"What will happen?" I asked. "Will the East secede?"

"No one knows. If it does I can go there, or I can stay. These people do not like us, but they will not kill us like the Northerners."

"There might be war."

"It doesn't matter. We Ibos will win, you will see."

We churned on toward shore, past the torch, the water spraying a little on deck. "Boss, there is a girl in Warri I must take you to. You will like her."

"How much money shall I give her?" I was alluding to the girl he had taken me to meet in Escravoes, for when I left her house she had demanded two pounds.

He laughed wildly. "Na-wha, no, no. Do not worry. She is not like the other one. You will see, no prostitute."

"Neither was the girl in Escravoes."

"Yes, but I had not known her in a long time. I did not know how she had become. This one is much nicer. Only if you like her, you can give her some shillings as a gift."

I told him okay, and he was delighted. "She is young, very young, but you will be okay with her. We will go to the house together. You must know our girls."

He turned toward the water again, and I roamed on back to the bridge. The night we reached port, he waited for me on deck until I was ready to go. Simpson stood at the bow and eyed us suspiciously as we left. I wasn't too enthusiastic about the idea myself. Pius had told me several times that the girl was young and I imagined us arriving at her house, the neighborhood out and gawking at the white caller, the family collected in the sitting room. I asked Pius if he was sure this was a good idea.

"Oh yes, yes. You will see. I have already sent word that we will come. We will sleep there tonight?"

"Sleep there? What about her family?"

"No worry. I would not take you to her father's house. She is staying with her uncle. Her home is in the East. She is an Ibo like me."

It was after dark when we got to the house. It was in an opposite end of Warri from my apartment, less prosperous, with no paving on the streets. The house itself was made of mud, crammed in a labyrinth of compounds off an alleylike street. It was hard to see in the dark, and Pius led me into the compound, around open drains and through winding passageways until we were at the right place.

There were two girls, both waiting in the front room, a dimly lit corridor affair just barely furnished. They were very young, no more than sixteen or seventeen, dressed in tight European minidresses. Pius spoke to them in Ibo, and both giggled wildly. Their eyes seemed glazed with laughter in the dark room. With this and the girlish abandonment of their giggling, quiet giggling but almost hysterical, uncontrollable, the giggling of pleasure, I was sure that they had been smoking Indian hemp. I felt like having some, but I had never discussed it with Pius and I said nothing.

Pius pushed one of them next to me. He handled himself like a master of ceremonies. "This is Janet. She will be your wife tonight."

There was more laughter and the girl snuggled up beside me. She was very small and very shy. Her age excited me. A slightly depraved thrill—the dark, drugged little girl, the musty room somewhere in the squalid maze of a native compound. The feeling of being in a lost den, far removed from the daylight world.

Pius carried on a monologue conversation with the room at large. "This is Warri, boss. You do not see it from the European hotels."

His remark echoed in my mind throughout the night and on into the coming days. It was not just a boast or a careless comment; instead it keynoted how much I did not know about this place, this breathing world that coexisted with the white man, a world that neither depended on him nor presented itself to him, secret to the outsider, more complex and alive than met the eye.

I hardly slept at all. We lay on a mat set on a kind of raised platform in the corner of a back room. She made love gently, submissively, and really only spoke once. I had started to use a rubber, and she berated me for this, violently upset, telling me that she had a mother and was not a prostitute.

But this incident passed and we clung to one another in the night. There was no ceiling and I gazed up at the wooden rafters and the high tin roof that I could not see, kept awake by the noise of harmless lizards scampering along the tops of the walls. The girl was soft and hot-skinned and passive and loving, but it was an uncomfortable night on the hard mat, the lizards going wild above.

We left very early, in the first white dawn, after meeting the uncle and dashing him cigarettes. Always in Nigeria there was the dash—a tip of sorts, sometimes a bribe, depending on the circumstances; but it was always the same word, always dash, any time you gave anything to anyone, an ingrained, neutral part of dealing with people. The girl caught me by the sleeve while Pius still talked to the uncle, and she wanted it too. The words: "Dash me now. Give me money." I turned to Pius, but he was still talking, so I gave the girl who wasn't a prostitute a pound note.

We walked to a main street. The native city was already awake—sweeping, cooking, radios playing, children around the compounds, women trekking to market.

"Did you like her?" Pius asked.

"Yes, but I thought you said she wasn't a prostitute."

He looked puzzled. "But she isn't."

"She wanted money, so I gave her a pound." I wasn't annoyed, just confused.

He looked at me a minute and burst out laughing. "You gave her a pound?"

"Yes."

He tried to keep a straight face, but could not restrain his laughter. He finally managed to control his amusement. "Why, boss?"

"She asked, when you were talking to the uncle."

This sent him off again, and it was a moment or so before he was able to talk. "But, boss, that does not mean that you have to pay. Of course they will ask."

I shrugged my shoulders and smiled myself. "Your customs confuse me. How is it that you tell a prostitute from a girl friend?"

"You will only find prostitutes in the hotels," he said seriously. "Otherwise they are the same. They are both girls."

"It is different in America. This is new to me."

"How can it be new? Does not the husband support the wife in America? Does that make her a prostitute? Prostitutes and wives and girl friends are all the same; the man still pays. I give my wife money, I give my girl friends money, I give hotel girls money—what is the difference? The only thing is not to give just because they ask."

"I'm beginning to learn."

He laughed again. "It's okay, though. That girl is nice, very quiet. Will you see her again?"

"I told her to come to my flat."

"That's good. You will see how nice our girls are. When I get to America, you must help me to know your people."

"What if you went to America?" I said.

"Yes?"

"It's very different. Don't you worry?"

"Why should I worry, boss? Do you worry here? America is only people. We are all the same."

We didn't discuss it further. I was tired and bleary-eyed in the morning, still absorbed in the experience of the night, the sensation of delving into the guts of the city, those inner guts that lived without me and that I never saw. I caught a taxi to my apartment and went to sleep.

It is late, maybe midnight, maybe later, and I am sitting alone in my apartment—sitting at the dining table, where I am fixing a cigarette of Indian hemp. I empty the tobacco from a regular filter-tip, careful not to tear the paper. When the tobacco is out, I begin filling it with the weed, packing it in with a matchstick.

I have been ashore all day and it has been a hectic afternoon, not with work or hurry, but hectic with people—drinking beer and listening to the jukebox at the Ijoto, the barroom banter of motor park boys.

"Jimmy, Jimmy, one cigarette for me. Hey, Jimmy, are you from the ship?"

Drinking too much and coming home to an exhausting conversation with my landlord, who has been on the loose since morning. "And this is what I mean; Mr. Chris'pher. All about, all about!" He points his index finger to his eye. "All of it, Mr. Chris'pher, all of it!"

Opening a tin of sardines to make myself a sandwich, I cut my finger and wash it at the tap outside, women and kids around. "Na-wha, the oyeebo de bleed now."

Afternoon noise. I have given Peter the day off. He is having trouble with his wife and has gone to discuss the situation with her father in a nearby village. He breezes back about nine, breath heavy with native gin. I send him for beer before he goes home. A tremendous boom on the concrete stairs; he has dropped the bottle. Racket of the curious. The landlord's small-boy sweeping up the glass.

I get the cigarette stuffed and move to an easy chair—light off, a mosquito coil lit to cover the smell. The rich smoke deep in my lungs.

The wind moves the curtains gently. It is a clear night after raining heavily in the early evening. Quiet now, people settling in early in the damp season. Only a few distant sounds, a muffled radio, two voices moving up the street. The landlord is getting his second wind. He passes my windows twice on his way to the bathroom.

I listen to the shortwave, holding it in my lap, unable to tell if the volume is too loud or not. Moving the dial with my thumb. A million stations around the world, each movement of the thumb a new world. Very many worlds.

Beautiful, quiet peace of the apartment, curtain blowing, a crack view of the outside, light, brilliantly night, sound from the plastic box in my hands, magic from nowhere, from the sky. Sometimes at night you can hear drums in the distance, a native ceremony or a wedding. They remind you where you are, but you don't hear them often in Warri. People have told me that you can hear them every night in Benin City, but not so often in Warri, and not at all tonight.

It is hard to think in terms of a whole experience when each vignette is a universe. Pius, Perkins, Diane, the landlord, rednecks at the club, a British *t*, clean, staccato, the Ijoto, a Nigerian girl. When reactions around you are different, you are different.

I have left the United States and I am here in the dark room, unseen but seeing all. Must force myself to remember those States. "Me and my wife go camping every summer, sonny, and let me tell you this, first thing after I get the camper parked, I unfurl the flag, Old Glory, yessirree, and I'm mighty proud to fly it too, let me tell you that. Listen, when your ancestors and my ancestors came to this country, it was nothing but raw nature, wild animals on the plains. Indians all over the place. And look what we've done with it, son. Take a look around you and see what we've done."

I turn down the radio and listen as the nightwatch passes my window. An old Hausa tribesman from the north, white Moslem dress, prayer beads. He hits his stick against the metal banister as he walks, a signal that all is well, every hour or so. In between signals he sleeps in the doorway downstairs. Presumably he deters theft.

Wind moving the curtain. How do you get it back? How do you get it back? How do you get it back?

Diane turned sideways and propped the pillow beneath her head. I had been sleeping a little and the movement woke me up. Suddenly cold, I pulled the sheet up a little above my waist and rolled toward her, against her.

"You must be tired," she said. "You rolled on your back and went right to sleep."

"What time is it?"

"I don't know; still early. You don't have to go yet. How can you sleep with the noise?"

The rain was pounding, spraying against the window behind our heads, as if someone were outside with a hose, periodically throwing in a bucketload for good measure. "It's good that way," I said.

She kissed me on the forehead and put her free arm between us, easing me over on my back again, rubbing her hand in circles on my chest. The rubbing gave way to pinching, as she took whole areas of my flesh between her fingers, squeezing and rubbing them together as someone kneading dough, harder and harder. I winced with the pain, but only twisted vaguely to get away from it. She watched me as she did it, her head still slightly propped by the pillow, a casual, relaxed smile on her face which faded from time to time into a blank, emotionless look of preoccupation. I moved my arm to stop her.

"Don't you like it?" she asked.

"It hurts."

"So?"

I shrugged. I did like it, but I was embarrassed to admit it. She went on doing it, and I looked at her. Since our first meeting she had assumed more and more of a dominant posture. I did not really feel any emotion for her, any romantic emotion, and the way she handled me, teased and used me, made me feel guilty. But I could not rebel against it. Her domineering coldness, mixed with the innocent face, gave me the same kick that I felt when I saw her in the club, holding me in a kind of bondage so that I no longer felt like myself, taking pleasure instead in the way she trampled on my identity.

She moved her hand down to my penis, cupped it around my balls, the sheet off me now. She massaged me there, hand up on my penis again, working at it while it grew in her hand. She took the head between her fingers and began squeezing it, pinching it.

"Not there," I said.

She looked straight in my eyes, no expression at all on her face, no hint of a smile, a deliberate air about her, but relaxed and detached. "Don't talk," she said.

And then she pinched me hard between her fingers, pressing her nails into the delicate skin, suddenly, brutally, until I squirmed in pain, water flooding down my cheeks. When she stopped, I lay back, breathing heavily. She smiled. "Here."

And she moved her face down and kissed it and took it into her mouth. When she finished, I did it to her. And after that she fixed her head on the pillow again and pointed to the dresser. "Will you get me a cigarette? I'm dying for a smoke."

Early evening at the club and all the slime are assembled.

"I'll tell you one thing, hoss, that little mother can get away talkin' like that here, but he better not let me catch up with him back in the States."

"Tell it like it is, Red. I just about had my fill with these queers."

"Says he's lookin' for work. Shh-it, ain't we got enough sorry hands with these niggers?"

"That's right, Red. Here, have another drink."

"What the hell? You gettin' rich?"

"Shh-it, ain't we all?"

General laughter around the bar. A lonely feeling in my stomach. It has been there all day, an empty feeling that makes me want to collapse. I can't explain it. It's not like the loneliness when I first arrived, more down than that, a kind of death.

"Hell, hoss, thought you'd be home by now."

"Can't afford to, Red. Signed me another contract. Figure to put myself out of the country for a full two years, save myself four thousand dollars in income tax that way."

"I know the feelin'."

"Shh-it, I got a wife and two little bitty kids back home. Got about eighty thousand dollars saved up. Couple more years and I'm gonna get me a little spread and I'm not gonna have no niggers around."

"You know it, hoss. Nothin's changed with me. When I get back, I'm gonna get me a nigger bitch and screw the hell out of her, first thing, just so's my people will know for sure I ain't changed none."

Still the death feeling in my gut, a rock-bottom feeling, so far down that there is no place else to go, no place left to sink.

I can see the front door from my chair. Two helmeted soldiers with rifles stand on guard. They are all over the town. Rumors that some Ibo soldiers from the East have been snooping around in civilian clothes. The night before federal agents raided the Ijoto and held the owner overnight. The radio is full of stories about an Ibo plan to take over the region. Tension everywhere. Eastern secession closer every day.

I watch the guards. They seem nervous and out of place. The whole thing like an exercise that isn't real, couldn't be real, acting out roles as if in a film, but not real, too absurd and foolish to be real. The death feeling.

It was noon, exactly noon, and the sun was white bright, glaring, gleaming off the silvery water. The rude, bright metal of the rigs and wells. We had no orders on the wire and headed full steam for Escravoes, myself at the wheel, the straight, short line to port.

I watched the wells glide by at the sides of my vision, like telephone poles when you are on a highway, but slow, the unmarked ocean lane in front of me; and it started again—the anxiety and the fear. I wondered where he'd be on shore, where I'd catch up with him. Simpson was on the bridge, but he was quiet, puzzled at my preoccupation. No one knew what was going through my mind. And I myself didn't know exactly what would happen.

A Speculative Look at Diane

If there was anything noteworthy about her early years, it was the extraordinary, almost total ease and harmony with which she adjusted to the overall pattern of her family. Not that she was a perfect child, never into mischief or never disobedient, but there was no hint that open rebellion ever occurred to her.

She spent her first years in a small town in north Texas where her father worked as an insurance office clerk. The town itself was one of those hardware store and courthouse atrocities which seem to spring up in the middle of western and midwestern farming communities—fiercely patriotic and religious and offering little in return to its inhabitants except a quiet, isolated place for hard-working folks to raise a family and tend a small garden and keep the wooden-frame house neatly painted and the lawn trimmed in front.

Her parents attended to this way of life more adroitly than most of their neighbors, and though they were hardly in the upper economic echelon of the community, they were among the most respected and upright of its citizens. Her father's sedentary occupation had much to do with this, setting them off from the vast majority of farming folk and the loud, hard-drinking dealers in fertilizer and farm machinery who were the town's wealthiest businessmen. Her parents were not really Texans, in fact, but had moved to the area from central Oklahoma, a similar place to be sure, but far from being as identical as an outsider might assume. Subtleties of accent and experience separated them, and the father bore no traces of the vacuous braggadocio so peculiar to the Lone Star State. They were Okie, not in the popular and stereotyped way that people associate with Oklahoma, but Okie in their unassuming humility and friendliness, more accurately representative of the state than the word "Okie" implies, and though ill-considered by the Texans, a notch or two more agreeable and perceptive in all respects, with, ironically, a higher degree of homespun sophistication.

A certain scruffy quality about the desolate Texas region rubbed off on them just the same, a bleached-blond touch of awfulness and tastelessness which they unconsciously picked up from their surroundings. As a girl, Diane had had long, stringy hair, and even on Sunday mornings at church—that starched affair where she like everyone wore her best clothes and conducted herself with the utmost piety, as anyone would faced with rantings and ravings of hellfire and damnation as she was —even then a touch of cheapness, a touch of spoiled windswept vulgarity lingered about her appearance.

She had one older brother, much like herself, although not an inordinately close companion. Had they stayed where they were, they might have become old with the town, weathered in the kind of limbo reserved for decaying communities that didn't have much to offer even before the decay set in. But they moved to Dallas, and that made all the difference.

The big D. It did two things for the family. It allowed them to become urban. And it made no demands that their ideas, habits and personalities need change in the least. A split-level, ranch-style home replaced the frame house. A manicured lawn with built-in sprinklers replaced the garden. A concrete and glass business building replaced the dingy insurance office. New cars replaced pickup trucks. All-weather suits for bluejeans. Clean streets and bright lights instead of dust. It made all the difference. It took the scruffiness away; but they were the same people, and they still starched up for Sunday sermons of hellfire and damnation, and on an aluminum pole, in front of their house, they regularly raised an American flag above the state flag of Texas when suitable holidays so dictated.

At puberty she was a shy girl, but not nearly so shy as she seemed. Boys sometimes tried nothing with her because it seemed so obvious that she would say no. Those who tried anyway discovered to their amazement that she was not only a willing partner, but knew more about it than they did.

In high school her development flowered, and the demeanor of shyness gave way to an easy and deliberate kind of extroversion. She no longer had stringy hair, but a beauty-parlor permanent that never seemed mussed. And always new clothes, according to the current fashion, chic but never too flashy and never immodest. Her attractiveness increased. She was a cheer-leader her senior year—in all external respects an all-American, rosy-cheeked beauty queen: a made-up, brushed, lipstick-touched, bathing-suited, hot-rod, hamburger daughter of the U.S. way of life.

Her overwhelming looks and mainstream wholesomeness mixed with her growing sexual reputation; and she regularly stole hearts, played with the boys as she saw fit, preyed on them actually, picked and chose among them as she desired. She attended one year of college (Rio Bravo State) and it was there that she met her budding husband. He was the kind of prop that complemented her social standing, and they married quickly, children coming just as quickly.

Nothing that happened later made much difference. They became irrevocable members of that busy mass, long before anyone thought of calling it silent, and long before anyone knew it was such a majority.

six

WE ENTERED THE final stage of the rainy season, but it was no longer refreshing; instead dismal, and I longed for the sun and the heat. The days were consistently gray, with periods of almost steady rain. The fury had gone out of the storms until they were no longer storms at all, but windless, monotonous falls that seemed to come only from some universal sky, without direction, a dark-white sky that blanketed the land as far as you could see.

The delta land itself was gutted with the rain, and in places the water table was higher than the pavement of the roads, spilling over these roads in pools and leaving an obstacle course of potholes as it destroyed the pavement from beneath. Many of the unpaved streets became impassable, torn up beyond recognition into pools and gulleys and ridges, rutted and mashed until they were worse than if no street had ever been leveled. And everywhere was the muck and the mud, discouraging traffic. You wore mud boots and let it cake up because it wasn't worth the trouble to clean it off. A stoical, dispirited blankness lingered on the faces of the people, as they stood in doorways and watched, or sat with listless bodies and tired eyes in darkened rooms, safely dry but drenched just the same with the pale whiteness of window light. The whole city was waiting for it to end, like some strange, primordial breed waiting for the dawn of history.

Nor was I in much of a mood for going out. Liberty became a routine taxi ride to my apartment where I sat for long hours and did nothing, infected by the limbo trance of the environment. On one of these days Pius insisted that I visit an Itsekiri village with him. It was across the river from Warri, near Big Warri, or Old Warri, the original settlement in the area.

We crossed by canoe from an obscure dock buried between warehouses, both of us shrouded in plastic, but already wet, helplessly resigned to it from the start. Pius took care of the paddling, refusing to let me help, panting and preoccupied as he moved us across the flood. I supposed he wanted me to see the village in much the same way as he had first shown me his home in Escravoes, but his vibrant spirit was gone, and he was quieter than he had ever seemed.

Once across, we entered the labyrinthine bayoulike canals that flowed into the river throughout the delta—the back streets of the delta, more water than land, where dry pathways were impossible. These bayous were very still, lined with mangrove, the stark, dead-looking stem-roots jutting into the water wherever you looked, and high above you like the walls of a canyon, sometimes in the smaller bayous arching across the top and forming a natural tunnel. One bayou led to another; and unless you were familiar with them, you could not tell one from another. You lost all sense of direction, all sense of time, all sense of where you were. The eerie hush left you alone with your thoughts, hesitant about disrupting this silence with the sound of your voice. When you did speak, your voice sounded distant and new to you.

There was little wildlife in this swamp. An occasional cluster of fishing sticks gave evidence that there was some. Otherwise nothing, only the small splashing sounds of an odd minnowlike fish which hopped across the top of the water. Once in a while too a bird or the chatter of a monkey. Nothing else that you could see or hear. It surprised you, because you expected wildlife here; if not crocodile, at least a snake or two. But nothing moved.

We reached a land bank and pulled the canoe ashore. It was much higher ground here, without the mangrove, and the same type of rain forest that you saw inland. There was no congested village, but every once in a while an isolated hut or two with an interconnecting series of paths and long stretches of rubber trees, some holding the tin containers that collected the sap, others apparently unworked, surrounded by brush. There were not many people about, sometimes a lone person on one of the paths. They knew Pius and said hello, but indifferently.

Neither of us spoke much until we reached the clearing we were looking for. Seven or eight mud huts circled a large, ornate well with wrought iron framework and concrete base. It was a sleepy village with only a handful of children. Four of the huts were locked up tight. One elderly man was working in a shedlike affair behind his hut. He waved hello at us but did not come over. As remote as the place was, I was surprised at the total lack of commotion caused by our arrival. I asked Pius where all the people were.

He grinned for the first time that day. "Many work in Warri. These are their real homes, but they stay in Warri while they work. That man is working with rubber. He is the father of my wife."

"It's quiet here."

"Yes, very quiet. All of the people here know Warri. That is why you do not surprise them."

I was struck by the hush and the peace of the place. Warri might have been a million miles away, so completely removed did we seem from modern life. More than that, Warri might not have existed at all, much less Escravoes. There was not even the sound of a radio. But Warri was there, less than an hour and not more than a few miles away, and the people shuttled between the two worlds, seemingly nonchalant about the contrast between the two, as if it were quite natural to experience two cultures at the same time.

Pius took my hand. "Come on," he said. It was a common habit for Nigerian men to hold hands, a totally masculine thing to do. I was used to seeing it and not bothered by it, but surprised because Pius had never done it before. He had been around Europeans enough to understand our inhibition against this sign of affection. Like the village, he easily shifted between the two worlds. I was puzzled by the relaxed acceptance of this duality. Did they think about it? Did they harbor any hostility against it?

He led me to one of the huts and opened the door. "This is my house," he said. "Go in. It is all right. No one stays here."

It was painted inside and neatly furnished, very similar to his house in Escravoes, but it showed no signs of ever having been lived in. He pushed open the wooden shutters and I sat down.

"I built this place myself," he said. "It has only been finished a short time."

"Will you live here?"

He smiled amiably, as if living in it had nothing to do with owning it. "Maybe. My wife can stay here when I go to America. After I am a big oga, a big man, I can live here sometimes. We should have many children here."

"Do you want a big family?"

He giggled in his usual manner. "Yes, of course. Even now I should be having some. All Nigerians must have big families. Ten or eleven children, no less than that."

"So many?"

"Of course. It is our belief. No woman is good who has less than that. They should help with the work, until I am an elder."

"Then what?"

He laughed again. "I can sleep then and send my sons for

palm wine. Na-wha. It is the best time to live, but only if there are many children. An old man should not have to sweat in the sun. One cannot be wise when one must work."

We sat silently for a couple of minutes, and the blank expression returned to his face. Nigerians could sit like that, indefinitely, silently, with no sign of anxiety, no addiction to motion, and I had adopted the habit myself. But I rarely saw Pius do this, and his sudden lapse into silence seemed tinged with depression. For a while he was again a stranger, again the lonely, mysterious figure staring at a torch.

"You sometimes go to the bars in Escravoes?" he asked.

"Yes."

"How do the white men talk there?"

"What do you mean?"

"Do they talk about the village? About the people in the village?"

I shrugged. "Not much."

He looked away again, into the distance somewhere. "I am just wondering. I have not attended those places and I don't know how it is, how they think of the village."

"Why do you wonder?"

"Because I don't know. The village people are not like the bar people. Because they live in the same town does not make them the same. I wonder if the white men know this."

He dismissed the topic with a wave of his hand and stared out the window. "Wait for me here," he said. "I must talk to the old man for a while."

He was gone fifteen or twenty minutes, and when he came back he motioned me to come with him. We walked over to the old man's shed, where I was introduced. He showed me some of the rubber process, how the sap was treated with chemicals to make it jell, then flattened in sheets in an iron press and bundled for delivery to the rubber companies, talking all the time in pidgin English that was hard to follow.

"The price for rubber is down now," Pius explained. "All the men here used to do this work, but most have gone to Warri for more money. Only a few are left. They do this and fish."

"Do they sell the fish?"

"Only sometimes, when the money from the rubber is not enough. Mostly the fish is for food."

It seemed an interesting, idyllic way of life, and I wondered if, despite the lack of electricity and other amenities, those who had crossed the river to the city were any happier. We drank palm wine in the man's house for a while, then started back.

Again Pius was silent, both of us fatigued now by traveling in the rain. But it was more than that for Pius, a peculiar melancholy about him that did not fit in with his usual personality.

When we reached the dock in Warri, we had to wait for a few minutes to get a taxi, but he made little conversation, mostly staring into the distance. He asked me if I had seen the girl he introduced me to.

I told him I had. "She's coming to visit me again."

"She is a good girl," he said flatly, "but none of them is to be trusted. I am having troubles."

"Troubles?"

"Yes, with my wife. I don't know what she is doing. No one knows what he is doing in this country anymore. Trouble in Nigeria."

He said nothing more about it, retreating into himself again, silent the whole way back except for a good-bye in front of my apartment.

I wasn't sure what Pius meant by trouble in Nigeria, but the political trouble was real enough, and after months of building up, it suddenly came to a head.

I first heard about it in the Warri Club. The Eastern governor was giving a radio speech the next morning, and everyone agreed it meant secession. The federal leader had proclaimed the former regional boundaries invalid and had divided the country into twelve smaller states, but no one thought the move would deter the East.

"It's fantastic, utterly fantastic. Roger says there's no way to stop it now."

"They're bloody well bent on having it out, that's for certain. Outrageous is what it is, after the years we've spent building this country up."

"But they won't listen, they simply won't listen to us anymore."

I got up early the next day to hear the speech. It was long enough and eloquent enough, like all declarations of independence, I supposed, even those that never materialized or never lived up to their rhetoric or forgot their rhetoric in old age. After the secessionist proclamation the federal leader announced a total blockade and economic embargo of the former region.

For the time being, it rested there.

Those were tense weeks, timeless then and timeless now, a time between times. An atmosphere of doom hung over Nigeria and it brought with it a sense of urgency. It affected all of us, even those of us with nothing to lose. More Ibos left Warri, fleeing to the new Biafran Republic while there was still time to get in.

Pius stayed and never discussed leaving. But his mood remained sullen, distressed. He kept more and more to himself, a brooding, lonely figure, no longer tagging at my heels or coming to the bridge. I decided he was upset by the secession and the anti-Ibo feeling; nothing much else occurred to me. I wanted to ask him about this and about the wife trouble that he had mentioned before, but he would not speak to me, except in monosyllables. I liked him and wanted to talk to him, but something kept me from really pressing the point—a slight feeling of relief. This I was ashamed of and barely admitted to myself, but there was a feeling of relief at no longer having him constantly around. I only half analyzed this feeling, the sudden pleasantness of being able to walk out on deck without him running over—not a snobbishness or coldness, more a sense of refound independence or freedom. I thought it was temporary, that whatever bothered him would wear off soon enough, and so I worried very little about it.

If Nigeria waited for war, slightly anxious and distraught about the eventuality, it nonetheless did so in fatalistic style, day-to-day business operating mechanically in the void. With no prospect of a very rosy future, these activities became more hedonistic than ever. The beginnings of the dry season accommodated us in this; for though it was not yet steaming hot and still rained frequently, it was usually sunny. The mud diminished and lethargic street crews tossed gravel in potholes.

The fatalism was contagious and I accepted it, forgetting trouble for the most part, in sun days and summer laziness. If any one thing remained as emblematic of that time, it was a new hit high-life record played on all the radio stations and in all the bars. The song was "Guitar Boy" by the Victor Uwaifo band, an upbeat limbolike high life, melodic and carefree, heard throughout the streets of the city. "Hey! Guitar Boy! Hey! Guitar Boy! Don't you see mama wa-te-o? Don't you see mama wa-te-o?" It echoed everywhere. You stood on the balcony and watched the scurry of lizards at the edge of the drying street below, and it was there. "Sing your song of love, Vic-tor Uwai-fo."

So most of those shore days I just hung around the apartment, content and glutted. As much as I drank in the past, I now drank more—not an evening drink or two and not a rowdy drunk, but a steady day-long intake, just enough to make everything hum. I smoked a lot of grass along with the booze, and on some days when I was free, I lit up as soon as I got out of bed. Wonderfully jaded, glowing days; the sun brought out the colors and always there was the music. Sing, sing your song of love, Vic-tor Uwai-fo.

There was time for other things as well, background things. An hour or two of conversation with Perkins. A quick trip to the club, a few minutes at the Ijoto on the way home from the market or the post office. A night at one of the European clubs, jazz and hamburgers at the Midwest Inn, the rock band at the River Valley Hotel. Peppered chicken and beer at the Green Virgin. Jeweled, crazy places dotting the city, always with the music.

I cut down on my visits to Diane and saw more and more of the girl Pius had fixed me up with. She came to my apartment, sometimes at night, mostly afternoons and mornings, young and small, her age making me experience a strange mixture of degeneracy and virility. She came early one morning, and we smoked grass together in the living room. She was shy about it, worried that the smell would carry outside. But I went ahead, not worrying about this any longer. Whoever could smell it had surely smelled it before now, and what did it matter? Which of my neighbors would ever tell the police?

She still does not talk much, not fluent in English and unaccustomed to white men. Her eyes glass over as we finish the smoke, the dream warmth, muffled pleasure laughter, her delicate body on my lap. "How is it?" I ask.

"Na-wha." Smiling.

She is very gentle and passive in bed, caressing my hair, exploring my body. I am easy with her at first because she catches her breath with pain. But her gentleness goads me on until I deliberately let her have it, slamming my sex into her, brutally riding her, giving it to her, giving it to her, ignoring her pleas to go easy, until I'm consciously trying to slam it into her as hard and deep as I can, until I am mastering her, abusing her, discarding her when I have slaked my need, and she is quiet, gently caressing my hair again.

It can go on forever, the glowing days and the music. "Don't you hear mama wa-te-o? Don't you hear mama wa-te-o? Sing your song of love, Vic-tor Uwai-fo."

And there is no need to think about it, to justify it or condemn it. No need to analyze and evaluate it. It is a total, mindless existentialism, caring about nothing, hurting nothing, affecting nothing, instinctual and natural, free as the breeze. And you feel that it can, that it should and will go on forever.

It was a foggy morning and we headed downstream from Warri to Burutu. I had just come on board in time to sail and was having trouble keeping my eyes open, so when the squall hit an hour or so later I was hardly happy about it. It was only a short rain, but strong, a last gasp before the dry season really set in, and it made the downriver trip difficult going. I had to keep a constant eye on the radar for canoe and small boat traffic.

Simpson came up and stood beside me, peering at the river ahead. "Crazy country," he said. "I'm counting my days."

It was a surprising thing for him to say, since he usually did not acknowledge that he was in a foreign country, or in any country at all.

Pius came up a little later with coffee. He gave a quick hint of his former smile as he handed me the cup. "The last rain, boss. Next week it will be hot."

"I don't mind," I said. "How come you've been so quiet lately?"

He shrugged without smiling, his face blank and distant again. "It's no matter," he said. "Take time with the river."

Simpson piped up when he had left. "What's with that guy anyway?"

"I don't know. He might be worried about the trouble."

It had occurred to me that maybe his distance wasn't a temporary thing as I had earlier thought. There were the unmistakable signs of a friendship fading. I was confused about it, caught between approval that he was no longer so aggressive and guilt that I was letting things drift and only barely trying to talk to him about it. Increasingly as the days wore on I found myself missing his aggressiveness. But I did nothing, nothing really to reinstate the communication between us.

"Red, you mother-fucker, I've been hearing some wild little stories about you."
"Listen, hoss, stories just naturally follow me around."
"Shh-it, Red, come on, let's hear about it."
"Well now, which story you want to hear?"
"I'm talkin' about that nigger ass, man. Way I hear it you're just punching the hell out of some smart cunt in Escravoes."
"I'm gettin' a little in the village, if that's what you mean."
"I could use some of that shit. Gettin' my belly full of these fat-assed bargirls."
"All you gotta do's take it, hoss. Just go in there and get it."
"Shh-it."

We got into port quickly enough and I cleared with the radio to bring her on in. I was too busy now to really think about Red, but in the back of my mind somewhere wheels twisted, once again setting the stage, practicing the play.

I brought her in until the bow was close to the dock, then cut the throttles and let her drift for a minute. The current swung her stern around nicely and we were side by side with the dock, but fifteen or twenty feet away from it. Double-screw vessels of this size have a lot of maneuverability and you generally "walk" them sideways into the dock. This is simple enough when the current is right. You cut the rudders full in one direction. Then you put one throttle full ahead and one full in reverse. The screws normally turn into each other, so that one is turning clockwise and one counter. This maneuver gets them going the same way, but pushing in opposite directions. The rudders are

111

behind each and stabilize the motion so that the only movement is sideways, one screw swinging the bow and the other the stern.

It wasn't that simple at Escravoes because the current messed you up, and it took me five, maybe six minutes of starting, stopping and cutting to get her in. I thought about Red while I did this, afraid again and more afraid than I would admit at the time. It went beyond that, and looking back I realize that I was on the verge of panic.

But I refused to acknowledge this then, only vaguely aware of it as I found myself thinking about weapons—automatically thinking this, as if my unconscious mind wouldn't quite accept meeting him unarmed. If I had thought about it more maybe I would have armed myself, either that or called the whole thing off. Instead I secured the boat and got on with the task ahead of me.

One of the men ashore told me that he had just seen Red in the village, and I left the area without another word to anybody. It was a short, very hot walk, the dust collecting on my shoes like talcum powder.

It seemed too as if I could not think. A feverish dullness enveloped me about the head and it made me feel disjointed, as if my head and the reasoning which ordered my limbs were something quite distinct from my heart and the queasy gut feeling I was finding more and more difficult to control.

I moved ahead like a robot, considering these things only as they helped to pass the time.

A Speculative Look at Red

He was born Sam Houston Miller, in Kerrville, Texas, the fifth child of truck-farming parents. The family resided on a small stretch of what must surely have been the least lucrative land in the county, and all of them working together were barely able to sustain a meager income. The mother was an almost totally silent woman, raw-faced and hard as nails, who divided her time equally between auxiliary chores in the field and household duties around the ramshackle house. She worked constantly during her waking hours and seemed to accept her situation dumbly, as if there were nothing else in the world but work and no other purpose in life. Once in a while she would say to the boy, "Sambo, when you get big you get off this land, you hear. You get away from this place and you get yourself a good job." But mostly she was silent about it, stoical almost, showing neither pain nor pleasure in her face.

The father was somewhat more lackadaisical. His manner suggested that he was constantly harried, worked to the bone, but the fact was he was lazy. He was fond of boasting, "Up by the bootstraps, that's me. Nobody ever gave me shit, not in my whole life. I had to do it myself. I pulled myself up by the bootstraps." And there was an element of truth to this; for if he had little, his own father had had nothing. Otherwise there was only negligible substance to the remark. He got up and went out to the field every morning, but how much he accomplished was doubtful. It was a small farm, not that much to do. Still he had to press it to get the seed planted, had to sweat it to get the harvest in. And there was other work. The house needed painting, the fence was unmended, the well dirty. The yard around the house was strewn with unwanted junk—discarded tires, broken toys, an old refrigerator, empty cans and bottles. But this didn't matter because it was up by the bootstraps, always up by the bootstraps. Every evening, after dinner, he sat on the porch and drank beer. He said a lot of things, but the only thing the boy ever really remembered was that one remark, up by the bootstraps.

Sam had just started the seventh grade when he quit school, finally quit school, after seven or eight false quits. Quitting school was a family tradition and it was no big thing. Quite the contrary, it was the only sensible thing to do. Education was a luxury that they had never quite understood or believed in, and the way they looked at it the guy that kept with it, wasted all that time, well, he had nobody to blame except himself. So Sam quit school, not sorry or hesitant about it, instead contemptuous of the fools who did not.

For a year or two he was the same as always, student or not. He worked beside his father in the field and began holding himself like a man, talking and cursing like a man. Sometimes, late in the afternoon, when work was slow, he went with his older brother into town or on long foraging hikes along the creek bank. They smoked cigarettes and drank corn whiskey on these expeditions, the brother consciously guiding him, doing his best to mold him into a fashionable, somewhat vicious country roughneck.

He had many fights now and nearly always won. Large and muscular for his age, he seldom hesitated about taking on some-one two, three, even four years his senior. More often than not he picked these fights himself, and that too was something he learned from his brother. Some days they waited near their old schoolhouse, a little up the road, nonchalantly seated on a wooden fence. When the students passed they yelled obsceni-ties, threatening violence for anyone who complained. They especially singled out those of their former classmates who they knew were planning to go on to high school, sometimes falling in step beside them and molesting them until they either fought or were thoroughly humiliated. "Queer bait," that's what they called them, so often that they began believing it, until they were surprised to learn that one of their closest friends was also high-school-bound. They said nothing to him, he was too big and too much like them, but behind his back they wrote him off their buddy list with a sardonic comment that explained all: "Shh-it."

He left home when he was fifteen, already calling himself Red now, and finally discarding the name Sam altogether. He drifted eastward, picking up odd jobs around the wells, mud carrier and roustabout. He was in Houston when he was seventeen and he enlisted in the army. Waiting in the induction center for his name to be called, he thumped his fingers idly on a table and belched. When one of the other inductees spoke to him, he answered with a simple "Shh-it." The word sustained him through two uneventful years, first at El Paso, then San Antonio, and finally Fort Bragg.

He noticed no change in himself as a result of his time in the service, but there were slight modifications just the same. The notion to drift aimlessly was dead forever, replaced by a clear sense of purpose. He had to make money—it was that. Money. He called Houston home now and went back to work in the oil fields, working his way up, by the bootstraps, from simple laborer to skilled rigger. The oil business was hard, dirty work, but it paid well. A few months brought more income than his father had ever made in a year on the farm. He began banking it, blindly dedicated to this one responsibility.

The Texas fields were getting crowded with workers and he moved to greener pastures—the delta country of Louisiana, south of New Orleans, and the booming offshore operations out of Morgan City. He wasn't especially impressed by the bayou country or its Cajun residents, but French names or not, these people were not all that different from himself. Not generally as well built as his fellow Texans, they were just as country and just as rough, if not more so, scroungier, grimier, cruder. He got along with them well enough, but hated them nonetheless. "Coon-asses." That's what the Texans called them and that's what they often called themselves, though with opposite connotations. No one really knew how the slang term started or what logical derivation it could have had. These Louisianans called black people "coons" but they were as bigoted as any Mississippian and doubtlessly intended no association by accepting the word "coon-ass" for themselves. So it was "these ignorant coon-asses" and "we coon-asses," and rice with sauce was "coon-ass ice cream" and the labels flew back and forth in such diverse ways that "coon-ass" finally became as meaningless as "Shh-it."

Red couldn't bank as much as he would have liked and he started taking careful notice when people mentioned the lucrative rewards of overseas contracts. He had zero interest in the idea of travel, but a few years overseas could really set a guy up. One Monday morning he walked into a contracting office in New Orleans and signed up for Nigeria. One of his buddies signed up the same day and spent a leisurely two weeks en route to the distant place by way of New York and Europe. Red couldn't see this shit, so he let the buddy leave alone, put a few more days of work in, then a New Orleans flight to Madrid, a quick change of planes, and he was in Nigeria, only barely realizing where it was located on the map.

seven

THE DRY SEASON finally hit the delta head-on. It seemed that
each boiling day was a geometrical progression of the intense
heat of the day before. Once again the skies were white-blue,
with no possibility of rain, little indication that it had ever
rained at all. The streets of Warri became more hectic and more
crowded, the noises louder, the clashing colors brighter.

But even this did not erase the sense of war coming, the
fatalistic, sliding disintegration of the country itself. The frantic
activity of each hot day only made it clearer that things were
falling apart. The troops were massing along the northern bor-
der of the seceded Eastern Region, which was reflected in the
midwestern delta only by an increase in police patrols at night
and security patrols about the town. The main action would be
between the North and the East, while the Midwest, though
loyal to the federal government, maintained a sense of neutrality. The region had autonomous control over its own troops, and
the governor promised that it would not become a battleground, that no attacking armies would cross it. The federal
government respected this position; and only indigenous, de-

fensive troops were being recruited for the region.

Part of this defensive buildup consisted of calling on military veterans to reenlist, and this included Peter, my cook, who had served in Burma during World War II. He took leave to go to the regional capital of Benin for this purpose, but he was an old man and I was sure they would reject him. They did not, and he returned to inform me that he was to report for duty in two days.

His leaving was very abrupt, and if he was enthusiastic about being in uniform again, I was skeptical. The day he turned in his key and left, I wondered if he quite realized what he was doing—if instead he had entered some romantic second childhood, gloriously abandoning his home and job and marching off to the barracks.

I had not seen Diane in a couple of weeks, and one morning I dropped by her house. The place was in a state of mayhem, boxes and crates stacked in the living room. The children were out of school and playing in front, while she paced among the crates smoking a cigarette. I asked her what was going on.

"I'm leaving with the children. The embassy says all the dependents should leave the region. We're going to Lagos."

"Are you coming back?"

She shrugged. "Who knows? It depends what happens."

We sat down among the boxes and had a short drink. She was preoccupied with moving, nervous about all of the details, and not very interested in the fact that I was there, finished with me in these altered circumstances. I found that it didn't matter, I didn't care.

"You'd think someone would know what was going on in this country," she said.

"Probably there wouldn't be any trouble if anybody did."

"I simply hate this kind of rush. It's bad on the children too. They'll probably lose a year of school."

"Maybe not. You can check around in Lagos. Things are probably normal there."

"I wish I could stay," she said.

"Your husband's staying?"

She waved her hand at me, irritated. "Not that, I don't care about that. But why should I have to sit around Lagos? I'd be okay here."

"I guess something could happen here. Nobody knows how the war will go."

"But we're not in it, that's the whole point. As long as I'm in this country anyway, I'd like to see it, not be sitting in Lagos listening to a radio."

"What if the fighting came this way?"

"That's what I mean. I've never seen a war before. I can't imagine what it's really like. I want to see what it looks like."

"People line up and kill each other. It's just like the movies."

"Then why shouldn't I watch it? Say they were fighting on the road out front. I could really see something from the front porch. I could watch them do it."

"There's nothing pleasant about seeing people die."

She shrugged again and lit another cigarette. "Niggers," she said.

I left a few minutes later, without much of a good-bye, not even a kiss, and I wondered why I should be saying either hello or good-bye to her in the first place. As I walked away she called after me, "Have a good time. I always miss out when something interesting happens."

Movement—unremitting, rapid movement. It is the order of the day. Women and children to the capital, evacuees from the East to Warri, Ibos to Biafra. The population of the city shifts before my eyes, like locusts seeking escape from the sun, going where it is more secure, more comfortable, searching for greenery and water.

I am sitting with Perkins among new faces at the club. He is not pleased with the trouble in the country, but he is unable to restrain his delight at the fact that the old patterns are breaking up.

"I've never seen anything like it here, not in twenty bloody years. People have come to this place and left this place as long as I've been here, and I've seen them all, all the Colonel Blimps and all the American cowboys, but never like this. Perhaps a herd of Japanese will move in next, after the war, maybe they'll come and rebuild the gutted city. Fantastic, this. It's living proof that there is no simplicity, no static absolutes, no good place here and bad place there. And this destroys your phony immigration, you must see that. It makes nonsense out of whatever you had in mind when you came here."

"Maybe. I don't know yet. So you're celebrating the prospect of war?"

A sudden frown on his face. "I said nothing of the kind. I'm simply here, telling you what I see. That's as far as I go. I celebrate no causes. But the war, no, I can't be happy about that. It's beyond understanding really. What of your Ibo friend? Is he much upset about it?"

"I don't know, I can't tell. He's been quiet lately. I've been wondering if I did something to offend him."

He laughs loudly, his rasping voice echoing across the room. "I'd call that a remote possibility. It's hard to offend an Ibo once he's on your side. In fact it's hard to offend any Nigerian, at least here in the South. Not unless it's something intentional; but a social blunder or a slip of the tongue, that's highly unlikely. How could you offend them really? This is probably the most informal, amoral place in the world. It's hard to break any sense of propriety when they themselves care about it so little."

He pauses abruptly, breathing and sweating heavily. He takes his folded handkerchief and neatly wipes his forehead. "Now in the North it might be a different story. You don't want to step on the Moslems. They believe in their rigid little systems. You can hardly say hello without following some sort of a formula. Strange people. Most Englishmen prefer it up there, but not me. This chaos you see around here suits me much better."

"Just the same, I may have offended him. He barely speaks anymore. I'm starting to worry about him."

"It's probably the war then. I feel it myself a little. It's getting to all of us."

He is right. It has come out of nowhere, possessing all of us. Everywhere you go the reminders are there. Everyone you talk to has something to say about it. People begin to realize how much they have anticipated the future, taken it for granted. Now the uncertainty gives them nothing to cling to and they are lost. No future leaves no present. It's absurd but true. And if each present moment depends on the future for reality and meaning, then what is life but an inverted progression, until you reach that final moment where only death lies ahead and all the past has only led you to this end, has only been important because it has gotten you here, like planks in a staircase which sooner or later disappears in a black, silent oblivion.

Perkins rubs his eyes. They are slightly bloodshot, bothered by the heat and his heavy drinking. "You can't live in a place and not be affected by the trouble in it. I suppose you feel it even out there on that boat of yours, serving the blessed oil. It must get harder and harder to make this place into a paradise, so how does America seem now, in retrospect and by comparison?"

I'm sick of his forcing this topic on me and I answer a bit stridently. "I don't think it's suddenly not so bad after all, if that's what you're trying to peddle. Maybe this place doesn't look as good and maybe the probability of finding a really good place is pretty dim, but that doesn't change America. It's still as bad as I thought it was before."

He chuckles a little. "Don't get alarmed. I'm not trying to badger you, just wondering if you've changed your plans yet, started thinking about going back."

"No. Why should I? I'd rather be irritated here. And I'm not contributing to the trouble here. I don't feel responsible."

"I know what you mean, but it seems like a strange comment to make. Sooner or later you'll understand me—you can't get away from America, not completely and not really. You just can't withdraw from it and stay there. You can't escape it, not unless you really go off the deep end, not unless you find a really remote place and get lost in every sense of the word, and you don't seem like the type for that."

"Neither do you, which makes it odd that you keep talking about this. Have you forgotten that you're an expatriate yourself?"

"No, certainly not. But I never intended to escape England, not England the idea, England the total sum. I didn't come here to escape it, I came here to extend it."

"Is that any better?"

"No." Chuckling again. "No, it's not, but that's another matter. Funny. You don't realize it, but that's actually what you're doing here, extending, not escaping."

His voice drops and his usual sigh of resignation signals the end of the discourse. I am very sleepy, always sleepy in the afternoons, and I yawn a little. Soon he is yawning himself, looking into the distance somewhere, over my shoulder, eyes sweeping the serenity of the river outside. "But there's going to be a war here, I'm afraid. No way of making a mistake about that."

The day the fighting started came early, altogether only a few weeks after secession had been announced. There was no immediate change in our lives, removed and out of the path of battle as we were. The radio stations spiced their programming with heavy doses of martial music and the newspapers declared that the federal army was advancing steadily. Editorials boasted that in a matter of weeks, if not days, the secessionist region would be retaken and the Ibo people "liberated" from the tyrannical rule of Colonel Ojukwu and his "rebel gang." For their part, the secessionist station reported, Biafran soldiers were bravely holding their own against the "barbarian" invaders.

I tried to imagine what it must have been like that first day as the federal army moved into combat. I pictured myself standing on a hill and watching the column advance to its first engagement, actually firing their weapons now, dying and killing, and me saying to myself, "So this is what it's like, this is that thing called war. They are divided into sides and they come together for the purpose of administering death," and I couldn't quite stomach or fathom the whole idea of it.

Those early skirmishes must have been as ludicrous as they were deadly—amateurish, hesitant actions between men not yet proficient at their task, not wrapped up in killing so that it had become a job to be done as efficiently as possible; instead scrambling and chaos and fear and flight, the normal reactions of sane men sent forward into something so obviously insane, not yet hardened or perverted, still rebelling against the battleground, still attuned to reality, sensitive to people and to life, not yet warped into good soldiers. Foreign journalists mocked these early fights and dubbed the whole thing a paper war of conflicting communiqués and propaganda announcements of victory and glory based upon only a few nine-to-five skirmishes, the taking and retaking of isolated villages, sustaining ridiculously few casualties, say fifteen or twenty dead per day, hardly worth calling a war.

It soon became apparent that nothing very dramatic was going to happen very quickly. The federal army chipped away at Biafran territory, but the press releases became more cautious, and for all practical purposes the initial federal advances had stalled.

Tension accelerated nonetheless. A terrorist bomb exploded here or there. The Biafrans had a makeshift air force of helicopters and prop transports, almost totally inept, dropping homemade bombs off target which often failed to explode; but the prospect of an air raid instilled fear and panic in the Nigerians.

They put up antiaircraft guns along the dock and often opened fire at vacant skies, a nervous spotter imagining he had seen a plane. Police patrols and army checkpoints were more than doubled along the streets and highways. Paranoia ran rampant, and every remaining Ibo was suspected of being a Biafran spy. Along Warri-Sapele Road a civilian inadvertently failed to halt for a checkpoint, and a nervous soldier fired his submachine gun into the pavement. The civilian, a true-blue loyalist, was quite startled, though uninjured. But a policeman standing by was wounded in the leg by a fragment of flying concrete. Hawks advocated that the Midwest abandon its de facto neutrality and allow federal troops to open another front from the west by crossing the region. But the Midwest governor, Ejoor, resisted and the federal leaders concurred. Still, violent sentiment increased, and moderates soon learned to keep their mouths shut.

For the first time people became suspicious and hostile toward the expatriate population. The Biafran radio, angered at expatriate evacuation from the region and the lack of diplomatic recognition, wildly claimed that foreigners were aiding the federal cause; and when Britain began selling arms to the federal side, their anger mounted. The federal government became more skeptical of American sympathies; and when the United States refused to sell arms, the newspapers openly suggested that the CIA was backing the Biafrans and that all Americans were possible agents. As if the army checkpoints were not enough, paramilitary groups were set up, unemployed toughs who patrolled the streets at night, supposedly keeping order, but in fact molesting pedestrians more or less indiscriminately.

Yet, the daily routine of living went on much as always. The market bustled, the nightclubs cast their high-life rhythms to the stars, people bought lottery tickets, schoolteachers held classes, and the Warri court tried cases for petty theft.

With the oil business shut down in Biafra, Escravoes boomed, bursting at the seams with the frantic business of drillers and contractors and supply people. We were overloaded and we worked longer hours, shuttling from rig to rig and port to port. It was exhausting, this constant work, the hot sun shimmering off the ocean's surface, and we were at nerve's edge, too busy to relax, to assess the situation. I hadn't expected this sudden increase, and at times I felt near the snapping point, frustrated and tired, looking for something to lash out at.

Pius sustained his silence, his sullen withdrawal, the crew becoming more openly hostile toward him. I tried to keep the lid on, but I did not interfere and I thought it best to let him maintain his distance, not wanting to encourage more suspicion, more hatred, more rumor. In some ways I was no longer the master of my own ship. Circumstances seemed to overwhelm my control, and rather than cling to the degree of leadership I would have liked, I contented myself with the problem of maintaining balance.

A welcome day of liberty in Warri. Evening. I am sitting alone in my apartment, relaxed, trying to unwind. An exuberant banging at the door. Peter, in khakis, accompanied by two soldier friends, and slightly drunk. He has stopped by to say hello.

We sit down and he grandly sends out for beer, insisting that he pay for it. Silent Peter; he seems so changed that it is hard to believe he is the same man who was meek in my employ, and such a bad cook.

He is boisterous and introduces me to his mates, gleeful about his new status as soldier. Curious neighbors are on their balconies, openly trying to catch a glimpse of the spectacle through my windows. Peter swaggers, confident, proud of the stir he is causing.

"Ojukwu," he says. "We will drag him out, no more Biafra." And he makes a pulling gesture with his arm, a dentist or a surgeon extracting some particularly vile and cancerous growth.

I am somewhat stunned by his visit and numb when he

leaves. But I am no less apprehensive about him than before, when he left for the first time. Something comic opera about his new demeanor, something wildly wrong about everything that is happening in Nigeria. I feel empty and powerless, not really myself, in a no man's land in the midst of conflict, and irritated that there is nothing I can do, increasingly anxious to break out of my shell, to act, to accomplish something, to affect the situation one way or another.

It was early morning and the heavy white haze hadn't yet lifted from the river. We were at Escravoes and I had been ashore all night. Now, in the humid morning, I was more in the mood for a quick shower and a fresh bed than a full day's work. But we were due to deliver some pipe casing to one of the rigs, then pick up supplies at Burutu a few miles down the coast before heading back to Escravoes and on up to Warri. I sipped coffee on the bridge and waited for word from the engine room. The coffee quickened my senses but it did not get rid of the slight hint of a hangover and the general feeling of exhaustion.

This feeling lingered when we were underway and I was irritated with the tedious channel out and the murky morning fog and heat. Simpson slipped up to the bridge and he was silent for a time as we moved swiftly out to sea, past canoes and fishing sticks and into the Sea of Steel itself. "I just put fresh coffee on," he said.

"Where's Pius?"

"He ain't on board."

"That's odd; he's never missed before."

He shrugged and shuffled back to the bunk. "Probably overslept. He can catch the public launch and meet us in Burutu."

I did not give much more thought to the matter and before long we had reached the rig. The sun was out now, the steam of morning dissipated. I tried to catch some sleep while we were tied up, but it was too hot and sticky, and the tossing and turning only made me more miserable, frustrated—a sensation that things were inexplicably out of joint. I could not quite grasp what irritated me. I could attest to only one constant, the blazing sun.

That evening we were in Burutu, but still no Pius, and I began to worry then if something had happened to him. I checked with the crew but nobody had seen him the night before in Escravoes. As much as they disliked him, they too seemed a little worried by his sudden disappearance.

Simpson accepted the possibility of trouble matter-of-factly. "Who knows, cap. A guy like that, he could be anywhere. And his being an Ibo and all, the wonder is it's taken him this long to mess up."

By morning we were back in Escravoes, and I sent one of the crew around to his house. He was back in a few minutes, saying he could find no one home, and I decided to check on it myself. It was another musty, foggy morning, and my shirt was sticking to my back by the time I got to his house. The front was shut up, but women were chattering in back and I went on around. I found his wife pounding yams, but she only barely acknowledged me when I asked where he was.

"I no see 'um," she said. "He de go for Warri."

My head was whirling with the heat and lack of sleep. "Warri? What for?"

"He pack away. He go live with his brother."

She shrugged as if to dismiss me, but I managed to get the address before I left. By this time the whole thing baffled me. It was late afternoon when we got to Warri and I was obsessed with the puzzle. In my tiredness a wild frenzy to find out what the problem was rumbled and grew inside of me.

Once we were docked I dashed ashore and got a taxi. The sky was very clear and bright and it was another sweltering day. The only logical explanation for Pius's movement that occurred to me was the possibility that non-Ibos had run him out of Escravoes, and a slow rage at this Nigerian conflict swelled in me. I even suspected that the crew might have had a hand in it, and I was outraged, the outraged neocolonialist who was going to set the situation straight. The rage and the heat of the day went hand in hand, these flames fanned further by the edginess that comes from lack of sleep, all mixing together so that they blindly pushed me on until I was oblivious to all except this one goal of finding Pius and finding the truth and avenging the situation.

I found him easily enough, in the living quarters behind an Ibo shop on Market Road. The shopkeeper was reluctant about letting me in, but I forced myself into the room. Pius sat on the edge of a bed. His forehead was wrapped round with a white bandage, his face swollen with the marks of a beating. One eye was bruised and puffed and closed.

He was startled to see me, and he acted cool at first, distrustful and resigned. He refused to tell me what had happened, but I was furious now, almost ready to attack him myself unless he talked. It was the shopkeeper who finally told me about it.

"For a long time his wife has been no dey, leaving the house when Pius is on the ship. She is going to the hotels and getting money from the Europeans. Pius find her with one man, the man with red hair whose name is Big Red. He tell her to come home now, but she say no. Then he grab her to take her, but the red man stop him and he beat him and he beat him so. He leave 'um, no go back to wife again, no go back to ship. Escravoes no dey."

I am stunned by the story. "I could have helped you," I say. "Why didn't you get me? Why didn't you tell me?"

Pius shakes his head. "I could not tell. Perhaps the red man is your friend. He is one of your brothers. I'm not sure what you think. Maybe you already know what he is doing." He drops his eyes to the floor—not mystery man, not hustler. White eyes just looking at the floor.

I walk outside and stand for a moment in the sun. It boils out of me all at once, hatred and violence. And I ask myself, "What shit is this? We from the Sea of Steel, what are we?" And myself?

Bland, double-living, quackerish sort of fool. I am standing erect, stone still, sweating profusely, and people are beginning to stare. But I remain rigid, just standing there, thinking about Red, standing there sweating, and fuck them if they want to stare because I can see now that it's not them, not them with their dusty streets and glaring sun and rolling eyes, not them with their high-life rhythms and their troops shelling the Biafran borders, not them that I am mad about, but me, me and my damned juggling act and pompous illusions, and half of what I've been doing really, on the bridge, at the club, on my balcony, with Diane, with everybody else, me and the Sea of Steel which I am a part of and Escravoes Base where I take my orders. Quite a little group forming now, as I stand, as I sweat, as I hate, once again hate, purer now, slicing to the bone.

(Stand by the radiator, Chris. Stand by the radiator. It's warm here.)

So I walk up the street, so thoroughly soaked with sweat that I no longer care. White men loading shit into their cars from the cold store. It's banging to get out—is there a backyard barbecue in the house, a trimmed lawn? Is there a big paunch? Or is it all sweat, with the sun beating its heart out? Trying to get out, to get free of all that corporate, bourgeois, redneck—Red. I have isolated an enemy.

(Take off your shoes. You're dripping mud all over the floor. Take off your shoes.)

What other rectification is there? Now, now that it's too late. I am walking myself into a fury, bitter, upset with the whole situation, ashamed, angry, mad at myself. I must be boiling, I can feel the water running down my legs, some very dull weight racking my skull, but I have an enemy now and that helps some, that is the thing that is moving me along, sustaining the sun. I have been mocked, and my enemy must pay for it.

(Don't be mad, Chris. I didn't mean to hurt you. A heavy rain is pounding the sodden September ground. It is warm but very messy walking around. Don't hate me, Chris.)

I have to get out of this sun. My eyes are burning with salt and I am beginning to stumble. All of my pent-up hostility concentrates itself, gritting its teeth in the face of the scorching, blazing day. And my enemy must pay.

So I got to the village, and a few minutes later I'd be facing him. I had so built the event up in my mind that the real situation ahead of me seemed suddenly unreal. Perhaps it was an illegitimate mental quirk that motivated me to seek him out, as if starting a fight with someone was a noble exercise, an undertaking of chivalry. What had he done actually? Beaten one of my crewmen? It was not the first time that one of my men had gone ashore and gotten marks on his face. But in this case, knowing the details and knowing Pius, I felt guilty about it. To some extent I felt responsible. And it was Red himself, more than the particular thing that he had done. His scuffle with Pius had only triggered the disgust I felt toward him. He was as much a symbol as a man, and it was what he represented that I felt compelled to attack.

Even so, I became uncertain as I sought him out. I felt a little foolish. It was easy enough to imagine a fight, to say I'd smash him, to hunt him down like a high school kid settling a feud, to build this attempt into something important in my mind, but now, when it was about to happen, I worried about how it would be. Actual physical blows are much more difficult to effect than the imaginary, victorious revenge I had been plotting.

But the momentum and the sun drove me on, along with more rational motives. For it seemed to me now that I had been walking the fence too long. It wasn't a conflict that I'd ever anticipated when I decided to come to Nigeria, and I fell into it without being able to stop it. Having fallen into it, I felt that I had to carry it out. Not only because he had beaten Pius and slept with his wife. I hated a lot of people, but I did not attack them. And Pius was his own man, and no angel, no devoted, faithful husband. So it wasn't Red or Pius really—it was me. It was disgust at myself that I wanted to purge.

When the pluses and minuses were totaled up, it seemed to me that I had been a fake. A fake immigrant, a fake exile, a fake captain, a fake man. I had told myself that I was not just another member of the expatriate enclave, but I had been nervous about being ostracized from the community I maintained I was not a part of. I rejected all that Red stood for, but I had lived much as he lived. I had pretended that I was different just because I thought I was different. So I had to do this, and I had to do it well, for my own benefit, because I had been dishonest too long.

The violent moment finally arrived; and the exhausted furies of my hatred momentarily diffused in that climax, then regathered and focused on the concrete, cold reality of where I had been led—indeed, what I had grasped from the situation, where I had led myself. I still felt justified in my hatred, vindicated in my focus, but the moment itself seemed far from apocalyptic.

I found him in the Mexico Bar, drinking at a corner table with a couple of others. I felt awkward walking in and I hesitated for a moment at the door. I caught myself and walked directly to him, but I felt increasingly uneasy doing so, with the strange sense of fear and doom that accompanies acts hastily conceived. All myths of victory were suddenly gone now, and if I had been anything less than a madman I would have retreated, priding myself on my taste for discretion. But I had become my myths, and though I realized that I was stepping beyond myself into a very brutal world, I sensed again also the validity, what I thought was the validity, the rightness, the gut goodness that had conceived those myths. It was that—less a sense of righteousness than a conviction of self. I should have met him alone somewhere, on a hill, amidst the sun and the wind, I should have shot him in the back, but it was too late for that. My courage, that aspect of courage that tells you that you can win, withered and grew pale in that bleak room. I had created a gesture of power, now only a gesture, for I had dreamed of power that I did not possess, and I realized the absurdity, the futility.

Strictly speaking it was not the fear, not the muted panic tug of emotion. Instead it was the lucid intellectual judgment that I was in too deep, that he was big, that he could handle anything I might be able to fling against him. Perhaps I had sustained my anger too long—abstracted it, intellectualized it into structured, rational contempt. Blind anger can make one do anything, can in its rashness and savageness slit the throat of any adversary, overcome, overpower objective odds. But I unwound too soon, and the clear glass sheet of fact dropped between me and my enemy, so that I saw everything much too calmly for one who is about to start a fight, unarmed, with no technology, no controlled mechanism of power to depend upon, only the naked fact of flesh and blood.

We met in silence. Anger struggled with the fear, and I could not help contorting my face; only through so meager a symbol could I begin the dialogue. A slight expression of amusement glided across his features. The animal air of discontent, irritation, puzzlement that characterizes the strong as they watch the uprising of the weak.

"You stupid shit." That was all I could manage to say, the words choking in my throat, mustering all of my energy to hide the fear, to control the rage.

"Nigger-lover." He passed the remark as a counterman passes a shaker of salt. If only there were noise, less of an overbearing sense of silence. But defeatism brings silence—the silence of the ridiculous, the silence of the lost, the silence of the impotent, the silence of indignation smothered in fact.

I hit him. The blow was an act of will, not a volley of hatred. It had the limp, half-hearted force of a faggot fending away a public insult. He removed his hand from the table and moved back. My mind clicked and I hit him again, and again it was a weak slap of intellect, worthless in a realm of muscle and bulk and drive. The expression on his face spread like nerves unwinding, like a pancake growing cold and hard, a flush of whiteness, calm shock and confidence.

Then he swung on me and his one blow was enough. I never saw it, but heard it crack against my cheekbone. The blackness lifted just as I hit the floor. Three stern faces looked down at me and it was not so much anger that was reflected on them as curiosity and contempt. They were looking at something pathetic. One of them took a step closer. "Go on, get out of here."

There was no question of doing anything else. I was wobbly getting up and could feel the swelling under my eye. It was cut and blood ran down my cheek. Red stared straight at me, face still taut and stern. "You better be glad we're not in the States."

There was another "Get out of here" when I got to the door and a beer bottle, one of the big Nigerian quart-sized bottles, smashed on the floor beside me. I kept walking, still reeling from the blow, anxious only to get away.

I was half out of my senses walking up the street, but it seemed to me then that I was always half out of my senses. Why? Again it occurred to me that it didn't really have much to do with Pius. And it wouldn't have mattered much if it had. He died less than three months after that.

What Is Entailed

It was basically an automatic or unconscious process, a fluid reorientation which was only discernible after the fact, and even then only as the result of considerable self-examination. The larger pattern began when I was born, and how many smaller outward and inward twists occurred before this big one is hard to estimate. Undoubtedly it was, and is for everyone, a continuous, repetitive thing, similar to the steady pushing in and out of an accordion in the hands of a musician. I believe this current to be humanly natural, if not always "normal."

Also undoubtedly, it exists in some more than in others. Regrettably, too many squelch it themselves, whether consciously or not; and many others, more flexible and less inhibited, have this personal activity preyed upon by society. Society, ever reluctant to embrace that which changes or admit that which is inner and nonmeasurable by functional, objective standards, "treats" these people, as it were, and keeps them in line. If this self-deluding regimentation fails, society destroys them or locks them safely away.

Looking back, I must have been too violent to have been so confined. I went my own way, a way that often seemed perverse not only to others but to myself as well, with unformulated obstinacy. It was necessarily an antisocial or, more accurately, a dys-social path—not that I sought this for its own sake, since deep inside somewhere I have always wanted the respect of my fellow man, but because it was the only path that seemed acceptable to my dominant instincts. It was turbulent and some said it was sick and it led me to the sea; and when that was not enough, it led me to Nigeria.

I could have gone anyplace else, I suppose, but this place had the advantage of seeming the most unlikely location for a personal kind of fruition; and as it was hatred and rejection and withdrawal which drove me there, the unlikeliness of the place was an essential element. To be sure, I kidded myself, perpetuated a myth of immigration, the simple fact of changing societies. I worked at this and there was some of it, but where I really went was inside myself. I took myself apart and I withdrew, as much as I could, from that external and horrible game that had always made me hate.

The illusions of simple immigration never quite jelled. I was able to bury the inconsistencies for a while, but that was all. More important was what was going on behind the mask, in spite of this new game. And what that was was a dream-filled inner examination, an inner voyage which analyzed, dissected and purged those demons I had long thought I could overcome in open combat. This examination, this tearing apart, killed something in me, something which held me back and which needed killing before I could go on. Until I reached a point where it was time to put the pieces together again and come back from the past, from the dream, from the new sense of self that the dream illuminated, having realized something about the basis of that self that I had not conceded before.

I would have come back anyway, but the fight hastened my return. It annihilated the illusions of the dream. And I realized what I needed to do next. I needed to reconstruct the mask, the consciousness, the outer, and I needed to move ahead, free of those artificial, social chains which held me back. There was another, very important element about this movement and this reconstruction. It was simple, but elusive. What it amounted to was that I would never be the same again—a breakthrough or a jump, if you want to look at it that way. I would be new.

eight

IT IS RELAXING to move swiftly along a straight highway, a reliable mental lubricant. I let the small Honda unwind and it carried me like a shot through the forest. The road was narrow and sometimes bumpy, with frequent broken places where the pavement had crumbled near the shoulder. But I stayed beside the center line and was not much bothered by this. It was just afternoon and stale hot, but I kept moving and the hot air felt good rushing around me and heightened rather than irritated the feeling of looseness. Then too there was heavy bush on either side of the road and you could sense that it was there, feel the coolness, smell it.

I'd only been on the road about thirty minutes when I hit the first Biafran checkpoint. The traffic was backed up getting through and I had to wait some and I felt the heat too until it was too much for me and I killed the motor and took my helmet off. All of the traffic was anxious to get through and the people waited impatiently in the heat, but silently, afraid to complain about the delay. Mostly there were taxis, but buses and trucks too, all jammed full with people, their possessions stacked on the roofs. Most of the vehicles had palm branches stuck in their grilles to advertise that they were noncombatants.

The checkpoint itself was routine and there was no problem getting through. A handful of soldiers manned it, very young and openly bored with their duties. The only thing that interested them about me was the pack of cigarettes in my shirt pocket, but I didn't offer it to them, and, shyer than some of their older cohorts, they didn't demand it, instead confining themselves to the routine.

"Where are you coming from? Where are you coming from?" One echoed the other, a usual practice. Even when an interrogator was alone at one of these checkpoints, he sometimes repeated the question, as if it were some part of the military code, an indispensable detail, an obvious premise that said that no question was any good unless it was asked twice.

"Ora," I said.

"Where?"

"Ora. Sabongidda-ora." It was a small village to the north, not far from where we were, but they did not seem to know it.

"What work are you doing there?"

"I was visiting there. I live in Warri."

"American oilman?"

"Yes."

"What were you doing there?"

"Visiting a friend, a teacher."

"An Englishman?"

"An Indian."

One last hesitation, one last look at the package of cigarettes, and they waved me on. I was back on the highway, hurling once again down the narrow ribbon that split the bright green forest, and once again at ease, more accurately exhilarated with the movement. There is a simplicity about highway travel, and perhaps it was that which made it attractive to me. Since it was simple, it cleared your head. At the same time the simplicity of it did not imprison you. It could not; the speed, the openness, the freshness of the countryside would not allow it. The place you had left no longer confined, instead it became sweet or sour in your memory, but more importantly, fixed and static while you moved away from it, leaving its static qualities in the dust of your tracks. It felt good doing that. Whether you liked the place or hated it, you felt good leaving it behind, even if it was only for a little while.

Highway child. Is he any different from the sailor? Is the road any less vast than the ocean, any less unpredictable, any less fulfilling, any less dangerous? You accelerate toward your destination, race for it sometimes, but while you are on the road, you are on the road, and it's all one—it's all free and breezy and forlorn. The movement has a paradoxical effect—it stops you in the present, calls attention to you the individual.

Highway child. Sailor. Modern life is choking both, choking the beauty, the openness, the freedom, and leaving only a jaded vagabondry, the sadness of night travel, exhausted miles, speeding in the darkness. Until there are few oceans left that are not cluttered with metal. Gone the unfathomable mystery of a virgin sea, empty and wide beyond comprehension. And gone too the narrow unkempt highways cutting through primitive bush and the bush still close, so close you can feel it, gone in a blur of heavy traffic and smoke until the only thing left that is green is exit signs and expressway markers and one mile is much like the next, uniform corridors between tangled, sprawling, desolate heaps of metal and concrete and glass, viaducts and tracks, bridges and warehouses. And what traveler can travel these, these highways and seas, and not be only half of what he should be, a traveler of the night, pale and tubercular? Who cares? Not the people breeding like rabbits, building and tearing down, fanatics, an insane army whose camp followers are smoke and soot and muck, in all directions, in the air and in the water and on the earth. Who is there to care but the highway child and the sailor?

I thought about all these things as I sped along, sped south.

138

It was odd that my mind should be drifting like this, because my ride wasn't a pleasure trip and it wasn't without tension. I was in a hurry. The night before the Biafrans had invaded the Midwest, completely overrun it as they advanced on the capital of Lagos. We were part of the seceded region now, cut off, and I had to get back to my ship. But I wasn't alone. The highway was alive with hurried traffic, and you felt a sense of comradeship when you passed a speeding taxi, palm leaves fluttering in the wind, driver hitting his horn in a little salute. We were all in the same boat, all somewhere where we didn't want to be or couldn't be now that there was trouble, and we all dared the open highway in order to get back to our ship or our village, or away from these, whatever the case happened to be.

It was only a few weeks after my encounter with Red, but it seemed much longer, so completely had the events of those few weeks and the events of the last few hours changed things, powered up a new situation, a new struggle with new preoccupations and a new perspective toward the past.

If I had been more introspective, I would have realized, even at the moment that the fight happened, that the incident constituted an internal climax. If not quite a climax, then a shattering point of sorts, the final or semifinal destruction of those illusions of escape that I have already mentioned. For not only had the conflict been with an American, but the American had defeated me—testimony to two facts: that I had not (as Perkins maintained so often that I could not) escaped America; and, that I was as impotent as ever in the face of that which I abhorred.

But I did not enter into this sort of analysis until later. In the period immediately following the fight I only sought to suppress thinking about it, this denial being overshadowed by a strong sense of embarrassment. I kept to myself. I lived in limbo.

Now I was alive again, alive with the highway and alive with the urgency of getting back to Warri. The Biafrans had announced a dusk-to-dawn curfew and I was worried about getting to Warri before dark. It was only a little more than a hundred miles away, but there were some obstacles. I had to go through Benin City and later, south of there in Sapele, there was a river to cross by ferry. Most of the expatriates were evacuating, and it was possible that I could miss my ship, that I'd be left behind, stuck without any easy way of getting out. The highway kept these worries from becoming too troublesome, but they were still there, pressing me with a feeling of crisis.

I had seen Pius once or twice in the past weeks and urged him to come back to work, but he would not. So I went about my routines and my duties and stayed away from other people as much as possible. Nigeria still intrigued me, as did the hot night streets of Warri, but it was not the same. With my illusions dead I felt dead, and I was living from day to day, accepting the patterns I found myself in.

It was then that Perkins suggested I take some time off and get away from the delta. He had an Indian friend who taught in a secondary school a couple of hundred miles to the north, and he wanted me to visit him and see a little of the interior. "You're getting a much too lopsided view of things down here. Besides that you're getting listless; sometimes I think you're ill. A holiday will do you good."

Listless I was and I took his advice at face value, offering little challenge to the suggestion. I got a week's leave of absence and headed north by public transport—out of the delta and through the sprawling mud-hut city of Benin to the little town I had just left. It had been a quiet place, like peace itself, and I was well received by the Indian. He had a large two-story house outside of the town, and I rested there for a few days. The man himself was very soft-spoken and gentle. In the mornings he went to class while I relaxed in the yard or took strolls about the village. At night we sipped coffee and discussed the war, but there was no urgency about the conversation. All was still where we were, a relaxed, idle way of life, much different from the noisy evenings in Warri. The village was not unlike the one across from Warri that I had visited with Pius, though much larger and fully populated, relatively unspoiled by the nearness of a city or the influx of white men. Despite the freshness and the change of pace, I wasn't sure that I preferred it in any permanent sense. If there were no roughnecks spouting off about "niggers," neither were there any high-life clubs or restaurants, and by nine or ten the village slept.

It was in the morning, in the Indian's shaded side yard, that I first learned of the Biafran invasion. I had been teasing a pet monkey that was leashed to a tree when a neighbor came by and told me that uniformed Biafran troops had crossed the Niger River and were in the Midwest. But it wasn't until I got inside to the radio that I realized the full scope of the advance; for the Biafrans had virtually overrun the whole region in the early hours of the morning, apparently encountering no resistance from the Midwest army. Radio Benin, now in Biafran hands, called it an act of liberation, the Biafrans having come to free the people from unwanted federal control, and the "liberation army" was steadily advancing toward the federal capital.

Now, once again, circumstances rather than individual choice dominated my life. I tried to digest the full significance of the fact. I didn't really know what I was doing on a motorcycle in the middle of Nigeria in the middle of a war. This I readily accepted—the fact that I didn't know what I was doing. But it went deeper than the present. What really bothered me was the idea that I'd never known what I was doing. Long ago, when I fell into a transient way of life, was I really sure that this was any way to live? Any alternative to the little boxed houses of the suburb? And when I rejected America, was that hostility the result of any sound decision? Or was it instead an automatic revulsion that controlled me and limited my life rather than expanded it?

Was the idea of immigration to such a place as Nigeria a

delusion or an act of panic? What made me turn cold toward Pius, then presume to fight Red because of him? Was it anything other than an uncontrollable act of panic? If circumstances made us, made me what I was, put me on this highway, then how could any way of life be evaluated, be said to be acceptable or not? How could there be courage? How could there be mobility? How could there be villainy? Why live or why die? I was too confused to think of an answer.

It was midafternoon when I got to Benin, and the city was in a state of confusion. Traffic was backed up and Biafran troops were digging in around the perimeter. The checkpoints here were less courteous. A soldier in brown khakis and tennis shoes stopped me, a bolt-action rifle slung over his shoulder. "Where are you coming from?" He shouted it in my face and repeated it two or three times before I could manage to answer. He angrily waved me on. "You are the people spoiling us," he yelled after me.

The Honda belonged to the Indian, and I dropped it off at the house of one of his friends and went directly to the motor park. I was lucky here and managed to get a taxi halfway to Warri, to Sapele. At Sapele I took the ferry across the river and chartered another taxi on into Warri. As we drove into the familiar city, I was more worried than ever about getting aboard my ship. Many of the Europeans' houses on the outskirts of town were deserted, the expatriate evacuation already having begun. The city was filled with Biafran soldiers, and civilians lined the highway out of it, all heading to the security of their native villages. The transformation of the place amazed me. War had changed it, and everything else was secondary now.

As it happened, my fears were unfounded. My ship was in port and there was no trouble getting back on board. Evacuees littered the deck and the galley and more were coming on board. The mate who'd replaced me was noncommittal about my return.

"You just made it," he said. "We're sailing for Lagos in the morning. If we wait any longer, the Biafrans won't let us out."

There was still some time before the dusk curfew, and I dashed to my apartment, where I packed some things. I dropped by to see Pius too, and he was jubilant about the invasion. "It will be over soon," he boasted. "You will see. We are Ibos and we are taking Nigeria." He flashed his old smile at me as I left.

I found Perkins in the club—indifferent, relaxed. "I'll be sticking around," he said. "I have nowhere to run to."

And that was all there was. In the morning we headed downstream. Warri drifted into the distance, into the past. It happened suddenly, this flight, so suddenly that I did not give it much thought.

Seven idle weeks in the capital city of Lagos. The Biafran advance was stopped and turned back short of the capital, and sooner than anyone had expected, the federal army retook the Midwest.

But those seven weeks were long and timeless. As it became apparent that the Biafrans had failed in their all-out maneuver, I grew increasingly preoccupied with Pius. Why was it that he haunted me? My stay in Nigeria seemed interwoven with this one human being. It started when I first saw him watching the torch; it led me to a ridiculous, futile fight with Red; and yet it was unresolved, the story of Pius was unresolved. I could not explain why, but his fate was important to me. There was an incompleteness about our friendship, and I could not let it rest. I didn't know how much longer I would stay in Nigeria, but I knew that I had to return to Warri once again, that I had to see him again.

I wondered about Perkins also. I could picture his delight as he sat around the nearly abandoned city. And Peter, my former cook—what had happened to him when the Biafrans came?

Where was he now? Warri—half empty, under curfew; I could not imagine it.

But those weeks in Lagos lived in their own right. Lagos—sprawling, vibrant city of life. The capital. The lusty jewel of black Africa. Warri to the tenth power. I kept to myself in an air-conditioned luxury hotel. Sometimes, in the lobby or the bar, I saw Red and the others. I played the role of fool, of outcast, and I avoided their eyes and tried not to think about what they said behind my back. In the afternoons I went to the beach. Beautiful white sand and violent surf. Downtown for a peppered steak dinner and a glass of beer.

Infrequent reminders of the war cut into that rhythm. One evening I was in a taxi, and we were held up as a line of armored cars pulled out of an army depot and onto the highway leading to the front. While we waited, the driver of the taxi behind us jumped out of his car and called to one of the soldiers directing traffic. He claimed that his passenger had made a pro-Biafran remark on seeing the display. The man denied it, frightened out of his mind as other soldiers pulled him from the taxi and shoved him to the side of the street. He pleaded with the soldiers: "I am not an Ibo, I am an Ijaw man." The taxi driver was just as firm: "I swear it." An officer came over, but he could not control the soldiers who were shoving the man. Probably he had said nothing more than "Na-wha" on seeing the armor, but they arrested him and hauled him into the depot. To question him, perhaps, more likely to beat him, possibly to kill him. Hundreds of Ibos remained in the city, but they were not safe, and the least remark or suspicion would land them in prison. There were reports of civilians hauling them from their homes and beating them in the streets.

But this was the war, not Lagos the city. Lagos. Is there any place like her on earth? Is there any place so wild, so oddly chic, so gaudy, so cluttered, so urban, so holy? Does Paris or London or New York have one ounce of her ego, her abandon, her chaotic beauty? Is there any place on earth more neurotic, more alive?

"Na blow the bridges when they leave now."

"No?"

"Yes, na true now. All the Midwest bridges no dey. Na Biafran soldiers na blow them all."

Whistling through teeth. "Na-wha-o."

"These Ibo men." A clicking with the tongue, like a mother scolding her child. "They are spoiling us."

"They should be finished."

"No."

"Yes. Finish them now. They are bad people."

General silence around the table. Fury and indignation tempered by inhibition. High-life record in the background. The muggy evening heat of Lagos. Sing, sing your song of love, Vic-tor Uwai-fo.

Warri was miserably, stinking hot when I got back there. The Biafran retreat and the movement of the federal army into the Midwest was coupled with rumors of the massacre of remaining Ibo civilians. According to the stories five hundred were killed in Warri alone. I could not imagine this, not here in this city that I had so heartily adopted. I liked its people—could it be possible that they were killers? It revolted me and I could not accept it.

Nonetheless the last few days in Lagos and the days getting back to Warri were racked with fears of what I would find, of what had happened, of Pius. I felt excessively sentimental toward him now and thoroughly regretted the half-hearted way I had responded to him. I realized now what intrigued me about him. I pictured him looking at the Escravoes torch and I realized what I had always wanted to do. I wanted to run up to him and grab him by the shoulders and shout at him, shout no to him. Not this. Turn away from the torch. There must be some better way, but not this.

So it was steaming hot and I was back in Warri. The parched city stank with the smell of garbage rotting in the drainage ditches. It bore little signs of war. If anything, it was more spirited, more carefree than usual. Women went to market and overheated taxis whipped up the dust. At night there was no wind, and the heat only settled around the bustling hotels and nightclubs.

The massacre had been real enough, and the house where Pius had stayed was boarded up. Neighbors told me that all of the Ibos along Market Road had been killed by dissident soldiers and marauding bands of civilian toughs. The street had been too full of bodies for cars to pass and they had rotted there for two days before order was restored and someone had hauled them away.

A woman storekeeper across the way remembered Pius in particular. "Na dead," she said, and she reenacted how he had been dragged from the house and beaten about the head and shoulders by the mob, and she showed me the place in the street where he finally fell and died, elaborate sign language to demonstrate how his blood had run from his body and dried in the sand.

(A little massacre, a little pogrom. Na finish them now. Finish Pius, finish Red. Na finish them now. And sing, sing your song of love, Vic-tor Uwai-fo. Yes, by all means, sing your song of love, Vic-tor Uwai-fo. Na dead now, na dead. Finish. Na-wha, it is better to suffer with air-conditioning than to suffer without air-conditioning. Isn't that right, hoss? Where have all the torches gone, where have all the torches, where have all the . . . When he is an elder, a big oga, a big man, he will sit in the shade and drink palm wine and be wise. Call out the guard, that's what I say. Where have all the torches gone, where have all the torches, where have all the . . . Sing, sing your song of love, Vic-tor Uwai-fo.)

I stood for a second and looked at the spot. No real thoughts occurred to me. I went up the street to the Government Workers Club and had a drink.

"Hey, whadda you know, hoss?" A tremendous amount of back-slapping.

"Shh-it, Red, when you get back?"

"Just today. They tell me these niggers were really killing each other around here for a while."

"They shouldn't have stopped so soon. It's hell gettin' back to work in this sun."

Horse laughter. "I never did know a nigger that had any sense."

"Shh-it, Red."

The killings stuck with me and I could not put them to rest. It was hard to accept that they had happened along these streets that I knew so well. It was hard to accept that they were real. That people killed people, that the bodies piled up and were carted away—that human lives were disposed of so simply. It made life itself seem insignificant.

Nor could Perkins be matter-of-fact about what had happened; no terse explanations, no words of wisdom. I sat in his tiny apartment and we discussed it, but we concluded nothing.

Outside it was dry and cool and the haze of harmattan had descended on the delta, indifferent to everything that happened below. The invigorating autumn smell of it seemed too pure, too good for the men who lived under it. Nor did the sky anywhere seem much consolation in the face of the creatures who roamed and ruled the planet itself. The creatures who raped the earth, who fouled the air and dirtied the water, and killed each other on top of this.

Perkins shifted uncomfortably in his chair. "I suppose you'll finally leave now."

"Why? Because of the war?"

"Because of everything. You haven't been the same since you fought the oilman."

"I screwed it up pretty good," I said.

"Why do you say that?"

"I didn't know what I was doing. Everything came to a head and I was outraged, but I only made a fool out of myself. It was like daydreams I used to have back in the States. My mind was full of culprits and in my imagination I used to put them up against walls and execute them. I suppose I thought that's what I was going to do with Red."

"It wasn't a bad thing to try."

"There wasn't any way I could have beaten him."

"You tried," he said. "It doesn't seem foolish to me. I wish I had the courage to do it. You live when you try."

Try. Na-wha. Na-try-o. The Nigerians said it all the time, but without patronization, sometimes as a compliment, sometimes a simple comment.

"But you've been right all along about me leaving. Even without the fight, staying here forever wouldn't be any good. The bad things here are just as bad as the bad things I left behind in the States. So it wouldn't be a good trade, unless I just stayed aloof. Some people say that's the answer, but I can't do it."

Try. Na-wha. Na-try-o. I am looking at Perkins, but daydreaming. He thinks I am accusing him of apathy. "I've never told you that," he says. "I'll go on staying here, but I'm only aloof to the extent that I have to be."

"I didn't mean it that way. I just wonder where it'll ever end. All Nigeria seems trapped, rushing toward Escravoes; and America already there, but trapped just the same. But this is only one dangerous myth. Even without it there'd be war in the world and crime and hunger and oppression and injustice. Men prey on each other. That's how they satisfy themselves. So how can it end? Is there a magic word, a magic answer that screens out trouble? I don't know the formula."

He gives me one of his philosophical chuckles. "You seem to do okay. The only magic is life itself. No life, no trouble. No trouble, no life."

I am annoyed. "Fatalism is too paltry, it doesn't answer anything at all."

"It's not supposed to."

"No, it's not. That's what's wrong with it."

He arches his eyebrows, waiting for more explanation, but I have no more to give.

nine

TWO MONTHS LATER I left Nigeria. I was just an expatriate there, and it wasn't enough being an expatriate. What Nigeria did to me I cannot fully explain. Vague dreams of refuge were dashed to the ground, rubbed into the sand. I could not escape America—yet some flash of sun, some dreamy, hazy, hot, tribalistic remnant of Africa stuck in my head—altering, so subtly, the perceptual range of all my thought.

I took a land job in the Ethiopian interior—a desk job with an American survey company, jolted from the West African heat to a dismal, flea-bitten village 250 miles from a city. It did not seem much like Africa there. We were in the mountains and at night it was cold and the people ignored us. In the evenings I locked myself in the squalor of my house, desperately alone, with nothing better to do than stare at the mud tracks on the floor, the occasional noise of a hyena outside, in the garbage pit in back. In this drab village—a virtual exile—my only real solace was the pang of Nigeria remembered. Sometimes at night I could pick up Lagos on the shortwave, and I missed it and longed for it with a violence that bordered on despair. But I could not forget Pius and the war and the Texans, and I knew I had seen Nigeria for the last time.

I had already decided to return to America. Not to swallow it, but to participate in changing it. I had journeyed from hatred to escape to commitment. And this last, which I had always feared, now seemed the only viable alternative. In a world, in a country racked by division, on the verge of doom, in this country which raced to its own demise, led on by false notions of individuality and progress, the future direction of the human race itself would be decided; and the repercussions of what went on here were too global to run away from, too strong to be ignored, too powerful to be flaunted, too entrenched to be overturned by violence in the streets. I committed myself to a revolution of ideas, the propagation of a new myth which would have no room for bloodshed or oppression or usury, a cultural revolution, and any other type of revolution seemed reactionary to me. I could not rule out the use of force as a last resort, but the use of force which fails and does not represent the cultural winds of change is nonsense, and very dangerous nonsense. I dedicated myself to no ideology except the ideology of fact, and fact is illuminated only by awareness, and awareness is vague and illusive and fallible. Admitting these things made it impossible for me to formulate any ruling mathematical proposition. But I would work toward this.

Just the same, this change in attitude represented no fixed destination for me, no rigid new doctrine. I could not delude myself into thinking that change would ever stop or ever need to stop. And I guessed that my intention to remain an American did little to contradict my intention to remain a sailor. For I certainly envisioned new trips and new places and new conclusions.

My Ethiopian contract neared its end, and one afternoon I returned home from work to find a letter from Perkins. The old man complained of the sweltering heat and the inferiority of

151

non-Ibo workers and the war which it seemed would never end. In a postscript he told me that Red was dead. He had been killed late one night at an army checkpoint on the outskirts of Warri. The soldier had wanted to search him, but Red was drunk and refused. He shoved the soldier and started to walk away. Then the soldier plunged his bayonet deep into Red's belly.

(Sing, sing your song of love, Vic-tor Uwai-fo.)

I sat for a long time in my living room. The radio was on, playing East African high life. I shivered a few times and felt a sensation of pressure in my sinuses, similar to a swallowed yawn, but rising through my arteries to the inside of my head, bringing water to my eyes. As the pressure subsided, a slow warmth engulfed my body.

I noticed that the music seemed amplified and directionless. It permeated the room and seemed to flow from all of the walls around me. With it my visual perception of the room also altered. The room and the furniture merged with myself and became an extension of myself. Continuous movement pulsed around me. As I breathed, the room breathed. As I turned my head, the room turned. Distance expanded and retracted. In one instant I was a few inches from the opposite wall; in another, the wall was yards away.

(A massive valley full of people kneeling before a tremendous Buddha. Purple haze is the color. The smoke of incense. Very loud, vibrant music. The worshipers are clapping their palms against their thighs to the beat, a rapid beat that makes it impossible for them to do anything else. They are dressed in silkish pink frocks, beating to the rhythm, beating on into the night, surrounded by flickering torchlight. And it is good.)

For a moment I forgot who I was. For a moment I was nobody. I had no mind. I was part of the room. Breathing. Breathing room.

(A highway child, roughly shod, flying across the plains. He is as free as the wind, only as free as the wind, but no less free than the wind. If he feels like getting drunk and yelling like a cow-boy, he will do so. And it is good.)

An orgastic rush filled my body and I squirmed in my chair. I felt that I was sliding off it and I put my hand on the armrest, but the armrest was flowing like water and it flowed over my hand. The skin on the hand itself had become transparent and I could observe the blood pulsing through the veins and the movement of the tissue which was wreathing with life. And I noticed the rise and fall of my chest and it seemed distant from me.

(Two lovers kiss, a baby cries, a snake cuts its path through the grass. And it is good.)

The room was alive, that was very clear. And though for a moment the mud spots on the floor would suddenly change into thousands of black, moving insects, or the patterns on the wall-paper would spin like pinwheels, or colors would change— cascading into falls of turquoise and pink—the predominant fact was that the room was alive.

(In the autumn we were astounded by the changing, falling leaves. Everything seemed golden, bright, Indian summer. My sister asked me why it was so beautiful when it was dying.)

So I sit and I dream of dark, hot nights in Warri. I dream of the river flowing past the cool of the expatriate club. I dream of music in smoky, sparkling high-life bars. I dream of the ghost of morning. I dream of entering firm black flesh. I dream of bright clothing and the noise of motorbikes. I dream of pound-ing rain and the silent domination of the yellow sun and explod-ing green. And I think of the people.

I think also, bitterly, with revulsion, about American heroes and car dealers and soap commercials and white starched stuffed shirts. And I wonder where I will be a year later—for I know, being a sailor, that I will be somewhere. It may be In-diana or it may be Innsbruck, but it will be all the same to me if it is warm at the end of the day, and if my coming is celebrated with the roasting of pigs on open fires and the sweetest and coolest of red wines, and the stamping of feet and the resounding of drums late into the midnight night—until morning finds me silent and at peace, worshiping the day.

74 75 76 77 10 9 8 7 6 5 4 3